THE PARAD

Eric McCormack was born in Sco... ... ...
he emigrated to Canada, and at pr... ... ... Ontario.
In 1988 he was a Commonweal... ... ...ist for his
collection of short stories, *Inspecting the Vaults*. *The Paradise Motel*
is his first novel.

'Finishing *The Paradise Motel* is rather like taking your sunglasses
off on a sunny day and finding that the world is in fact much greyer.
It is highly recommended as a place to take your imagination for a
holiday.' *Literary Review*

'Marvellous, macabre and shocking . . . for those who inhale their
fiction neat and like it lasting, *The Paradise Motel* will prove
addictive, for it is that rarity, a tour de force.'
Scotland on Sunday

'Eric McCormack's brilliant and unsettling novel steeps itself in
mystery, horror and suspense to tell a story about the very art of
storytelling. Each character is a teller of tales, which makes them
all liars.' *New York Times Book Review*

'His flat wide-eyed magic realism, giving equal weight to the
marvelous and the mundane, seems to owe more, in terms both of
style and vision, to Garcia Marquez than to any of his countrymen
. . . haunting, compelling, irresistible.' *Calgary Herald*

'A virtuoso . . . the stories are both phantasmagorical and very
real, and McCormack holds them together with a sophisticated
prose rich in beautiful descriptions. The novel exhilarates.'
Publishers Weekly

'A gifted storyteller . . . a truly excellent first novel . . . an
entrancing tale . . . the plot twists and turns elegantly into a
tricksy ending.' *Cosmopolitan*

'McCormack is prison warden of our collective subconscious.'
Glasgow Herald

By the same author

INSPECTING THE VAULTS

ERIC McCORMACK

The Paradise Motel

Flamingo
Published by Fontana Paperbacks

For Nancy Helfinger

First published in Great Britain by
Bloomsbury Publishing Ltd 1989

This Flamingo edition first published
in 1990 by Fontana Paperbacks

Flamingo is an imprint of Fontana Paperbacks,
part of the Collins Publishing Group,
8 Grafton Street, London W1X 3LA

Copyright © Eric McCormack 1989

Printed and bound in Great Britain by
William Collins Sons & Co. Ltd, Glasgow

What, should we get rid of our ignorance,
the very substance of our lives,
merely in order to understand one another?

R.P. BLACKMUR

Prologue

He is dozing, sitting in a wicker chair on a balcony of the Paradise Motel. The squat, clapboard building looks out across a beach onto the North Atlantic Ocean, a grey ocean on a grey day. The man is wearing a heavy tweed overcoat, gloves, and a scarf. When he opens his eyes, as he does from time to time, he can see for miles to where the grey water meets the slightly less grey sky. Today, he thinks, this ocean might easily be a huge handwritten manuscript covered as far as the eye can see with regular lines of neat, cursive writing. At the bottom, near the shore, the lines are clearer, and he keeps thinking it might be possible to make out what they say. Then, crash! they break up, on pale brown sand, on black rocks, on the pitted remains of an old concrete jetty. The words, whatever they are, dissolve into white foam on the beach.

The name of this man, that is to say, *my* name, is Ezra Stevenson. I play a minor part in what follows. The principal figures are the four Mackenzies, whose childhood was mysterious, perhaps horrific; what happened to them later is the major concern. A few other people are important, too: JP, retired newspaperman; the man called Pablo Renowsky, philosophic ex-boxer; Doctor Yerdeli, Director of the Institute for the Lost; Donald Cromarty, old friend and scholar, who helped me in the search for resolutions (comforting word in an uneasy universe); and one or two others.

Not forgetting, of course, my own grandfather, Daniel Stevenson. He's the one who told me about the Mackenzies. If he hadn't come home to die, after a disappearance of thirty years, I doubt whether I would ever have heard of them. Maybe no one would. Most often, in the matter of individual lives, time, with implacable energy, wipes out those who would have been worth remembering, along with the rest of us. That, for me, is the sad lesson of history, as well as the great solace.

Part One

DANIEL

1

As I grew older, I began to look like Daniel Stevenson, my grandfather, who died when I was twelve. In the mirror, each day, I could see him in me. My eyes were green, like his. By the time I was fifteen, I had grown to his height and my face had thinned a lot, so that the resemblance was even stronger, as though his face had been hiding underneath mine all along, the kernel beneath the skin. Whenever someone else, an outsider, pointed out the likeness, my grandmother, Joanna, and my mother, Elizabeth, were not pleased. As for myself, I can't say I was thrilled either. For I had seen how the old man looked as he lay dead, and could never forget it; I knew that was how I would look some day, if I lived to his age, and died in a bed.

I only knew him for the length of one week, but during it, we talked and talked. I don't think, looking back, that it is strange I never asked him why he ran away from Muirton, thirty years before. Some children are too devious even to dream of asking such questions. He gave me hints, all along, without my needing to ask. He had a habit of not looking directly at me when he was about to say something very personal.

As, for example, when he said in his hoarse voice: 'Ezra, it's a miracle I left this place, you know. It wasn't planned.'

He seemed to consider that, for a while. Then he said: 'Like a squall at sea on a calm day. It just happened.'

Another time, he said this: 'Muirton was too hard for me, or I was too soft for it. I don't know which.'

And once, too: 'The sky here used to remind me of a tunnel. I felt I could never stand up straight.'

That was the kind of thing he might say when he wasn't telling stories about his travels. And he would use words like 'ugliness,' and 'beauty,' words none of the other men of Muirton ever used. He said he'd decided there must be beauty in life somewhere, and he was going looking for it.

The afternoon he told me the story of his journey to Patagonia, thirty years before, was one of those wet afternoons in Muirton, with heavy rain sluicing the slate roof and the sooty windows of the attic where he was lying. Perhaps the rain reminded him. Or perhaps the bone. He had been showing me some odds and ends from his trouser pockets: tin coins with holes in them, from Chinese tombs; a complicated knot in a hemp rope from Oluba (to untie it meant bad luck); some fragments of red Mayan pottery, a thousand years old (he said the red was human blood). As for the bone, it was a greyish colour, scrimshawed with a three-masted ship, sails bulging in a stiff artist's gale.

'That's how the *Mingulay* looked,' he said.

I was sitting on the edge of his mattress, and could just make out, at eye-level, through the attic window, the rain-distorted outline of the hills of Muirton, worn down by history. Or even if I could not actually see

14

them, I believed in them, I was sure of their reality. As he talked, I could smell his stale breath; but his beaky face was less yellow than usual. It was washed clear, for a while, by the flood of memories from that time, thirty years before, when he was strong, with the whole world in front of him.

2

He had signed on as a deck-hand on the *Mingulay*, the musical-sounding name of a small three-master. It was to carry a party of scientists and adventurers to Patagonia, the grim wasteland at the foot of South America. He knew nothing about the place then. Its name was only a satisfying-sounding foreign word in a school textbook. He did not know that the region was famed as a dinosaur graveyard. That, for decades, archaeologists had ripped open its surface to expose strange and massive relics.

Near the turn of the century, rumours began to spread, from the few natives left in the hinterland and from travellers hurrying through, that a live monster had been spotted trundling around the foothills, almost big enough to pass for a small foothill itself. Experts said it sounded like a mylodon, a primitive kind of giant sloth. Country after country began sending expeditions to Patagonia in the hope of being the first to capture a creature so slow to change that a million years of evolution had not been long enough.

In the end, of course, no one found any such monster. The sighting was a hoax or, just as likely, a dream, hatched by dreamers in a dream world.

So the expedition to which Daniel Stevenson was attached was no more successful than any of the others. But for him, the adventure was what counted. He had spent most of his life, till then, working in the Muirton mine. He had told lies to the leaders of the expedition so that they would sign him on as a deck-hand, and when they did, he could hardly believe his luck. Everything, from the start, was marvellous: the feel of a wooden hull under him, breathing and creaking and rolling; the salt-water smell; the secrets of the ship itself, a country with a strange language: 'booms,' 'spars,' 'starboard,' 'port,' 'bow,' 'stern,' 'fore and aft,' 'gunwales,' 'fo'c'sle,' 'topgallants,' 'mizzens'; new words to be learnt every day. He was always the one most willing to climb the rigging to the swaying topmast and the open sky. He saw himself as a bird, no longer a blind mole condemned to endless, dark tunnels.

The voyage was a long one. At night, the sky seethed with fragments of light; but even on starless nights, the ship's wake created its own milky way. In the day, Daniel would spend hours at the bow, watching the ship drive forward into the winds. The harder they blew, the more determinedly the *Mingulay* advanced. He felt a great bond with her.

But when the ship was, at last, coasting down the

final miles, how unpleasantly familiar Patagonia seemed to him, how the swirls of mist on the squat hills, the treeless swamps, reminded him of the country around Muirton. As though a trick had been played upon him, and his escape tunnel ended up back in the prison-yard. He almost expected to see, around every headland, the great Ferris wheel of the Muirton mine elevator rotating with the earth, to smell the acrid smell of coal smoke, and to hear the siren hooting at his failure.

The *Mingulay* anchored a quarter of a mile offshore, and the crew worked all day ferrying provisions. The surf was a great hostile machine that crushed the arm of one sailor between the ship's hull and the tender, and never gave up trying to drown the others. But, at last, just before nightfall, the provisions and the men were ashore, except for a skeleton crew left to guard the empty ship. On the endless white beach, the expeditioners lit fires of driftwood, and the cook made a meal of bannocks and fish-stew.

3

Those evenings in Patagonia Daniel Stevenson never forgot. Gathered in a ring of light round the fire, their backs walling out the night, the men would sit with their mugs of rum, telling stories as though they were still in their hammocks in the fo'c'sle on the voyage south.

One story Daniel heard there, in Patagonia, thirty years before, implanted itself in him with the solidity of the landscape of the place itself. The expedition had, by then, travelled inland for about a week, and set up camp on a plateau in the foothills. It was night, rainy and cool. The teller of the story was Zachary Mackenzie, the Engineer, whose job was to take care of the auxiliary engine of the *Mingulay*.

He was a youngish man, tall, his fair hair already thinning. He knew something about medicine. When Daniel Stevenson injured his hand in a ratchet early on the voyage south, Mackenzie washed and poulticed it daily. Often, Daniel knocked at his cabin door for treatment, to find the Engineer scribbling in yellow notebooks. He never seemed to mind interruptions by Daniel. Perhaps, he said, they got along so well because his own specialty was the innards of a ship, while Daniel had been intimate with the innards of the earth. This was as near as he ever came to humour.

Unless one other comment of his to Daniel was meant to be funny. They knew each other pretty well by that time, and had been talking about love, and women.

'I have never been in love,' Zachary Mackenzie said. 'Take my advice, Daniel, never put too much confidence in a man who has never been in love.' He didn't laugh.

This Zachary Mackenzie, then, was the one who told that story long ago, in Patagonia, his light-blue eyes like steel reflecting the firelight.

4

Up in that damp attic, all those years later, Daniel Stevenson wanted me to know he had never told anyone else the story.

'Ezra, this is the first time,' he said.

He paused, and said, 'Never before, not once.'

Then, after a while, he said again, slowly, 'Ezra, yes. This is the first time.'

Then he was silent, lifting a lid, peering into a box sealed thirty years before. His yellow-green eyes were burning. He remembered exactly what kind of night that was, who was sitting there (all dead men now, surely) around the fire in the Patagonian darkness.

I myself could hear the rain outside the attic slacking off a good deal. It was still telling its own story, but softer now, to the slate roof and the beaten, huddled hills beyond the dirty window.

5

The firelight was a brilliant incision in the great belly of the Patagonian night. Bats were wheeling around, in and out, and rain was whispering softly to the blazing logs. The hills had long ago disappeared.

The Engineer spoke up. He said he remembered something that might interest them, something that had really happened. He was a man from the islands who kept, in his cabin, notebooks filled with jottings no one else was allowed to see. His hands were familiar with bunker oil and heavy steel piping, yet he had the elegant fingers of a pianist or a surgeon, the milky blue eyes of a dreamer. He rose from his squatting position with the others and took the higher place on an upturned barrel. Then he spoke in a soft, northern voice.

'When I was a young boy, a strange thing happened in our town. A new doctor with a southern accent came up to practise at our end of the island with his wife and four children, two boys and two girls all under ten years old. The doctor was thin with a head like a snake. His wife was beautiful, with long, fair hair tied in a bun behind her head, and always happy, always singing. That's all I remember about her.

'After only a month, the thing happened. On a sunny morning in September, this new doctor came to the duty-desk of the police station looking very upset, to report that his wife was missing. He said she'd gone for her daily walk the day before and not come back. He had looked everywhere, not wanting to make a fuss. But now he was becoming very anxious.

'The police went to work. They made sure first of all that she had not boarded the ferry for the mainland, and then they organized a search for her. Many of the men helped out. They searched everywhere, day and night, for two days, but they could find no sign of her.

'Life had to go on. The four children showed up at school the next day as usual. But they did not look well. They were all pale and washed out as though they had been crying. What was most noticeable was the way they walked. They all walked stiffly, as though they were old men.

'The island children hadn't known them long enough, and were shy about asking what was the matter, thinking it must have something to do with their mother's disappearance.

'But on their second day back at school, one of the little girls, who was about six years old then, turned very sick at her desk and fell over onto the floor with convulsions, holding her stomach and groaning.

'The old schoolmistress took her to the staff room and made her comfortable with blankets and a pillow. Then she phoned the girl's father, the doctor, to come right away.

'The little girl kept on groaning in agony, and the schoolmistress tried to coax her to show where the pain was. The little girl was not willing at first, only she was in pain, and saw the schoolmistress wanted to help. So she began to unbutton her dress.

'But a car drew up outside, and her father, the doctor, came rushing into the staff-room shouting, 'No! No!' and lifted her away in his arms. He then came back for the other three children, and took them all away in the car with him.

'The old schoolmistress had seen enough. She phoned the police station.

'Without any delay, the sergeant and his constable drove to the doctor's house on the cliffs overlooking the sea. They knocked and stood waiting for a few minutes till the doctor, looking nervous, came to the door. The sergeant said he'd like to see the children. The doctor at first said they were too sick to be disturbed, but the sergeant insisted, and the three of them went inside.

'All the children were lying in their beds in one large room on the ocean side of the house, and anyone could tell how sick they were. The sergeant knew what he had to do. He asked them to open up their clothing for him. They all did so, with groans and gasps of pain.

'He understood the reason for their suffering.

'The sergeant saw that each of those four children had a large incision in the centre of their abdomens, the sutures fresh, the wounds inflamed.

'Their father, the doctor, who had been standing watching all of this, was sobbing quietly. When the sergeant asked him why the children had been operated upon, he would say nothing.

'The sergeant called the local ambulance and took all four children to the hospital at the other end of the island.

'The resident surgeon there, a kind man, saw the sergeant's concern. He ordered the little girl who had been in the greatest pain to be taken into the operating theatre where he had been about to conduct a class in pathology for some nurses. The little girl was anaesthetized. The resident and the nurses could see how pus mixed with blood was oozing from the wound. No wonder she had been in agony.

'The resident then cut the sutures and lifted them away. He slid his fingers into the wound and groped around. He could feel a lump of some sort. With a pair of calipers, he managed to grip part of it. He carefully fished it out and held it up in the air.

'All of those assembled round that table saw something they would never forget. The resident had snared in the calipers a severed human hand, dripping blood and pus. He was holding it by its thumb, and they could all see, quite clearly, the gold wedding ring on its middle finger and the scarlet polish on the long fingernails.'

The Engineer stopped for a moment to take a drink of rum from his tin mug. The night had turned chilly, and the members of the expedition crouched nearer to the fire's heat. He continued:

'That was how they found out that the new doctor had killed his wife. He had cut off parts of her and buried them inside the children. Each of the four children contained a hand, or a foot. Later the family pets, a Highland collie and a big ginger cat, were found lying in the house cellar, half alive. They too had abdominal incisions. The local veterinarian discovered the woman's eyes in the dog and her ears in the cat.

'The resident testified later that he hoped never to perform such a salvage operation again. He was sure that if the man had had enough children and pets, he'd have managed to conceal every part of her. As it was, a fisherman found the rest of her body under some rocks by the shore.

'The resident said the father's workmanship was a

23

marvel, though. He had never seen such skill with the knife. The murderer himself was silent. He was later sentenced to death, though his children pleaded for his life. The islanders would never allow hangings on the island for fear of bad luck. They did not object, however, to his being hanged on the mainland. And he was.'

The Engineer had finished. He was nodding his head slightly, as if to support the truth of what he had just said.

'I don't believe a word of it,' said one of the crew, a fair-haired man from London. 'It's a load of codswallop! As though a human body could be used as a repository of dead limbs!'

Many of the others sitting around the fire began to laugh too, with relief as much as anything, at the thought that it was all really a joke.

The Engineer slid slowly to his feet from the barrel. The rain was hissing down into the fire now even more noisily, as though the logs were debating the issue too. In and out of the firelight, bats were wheeling, one instant solid and tangible, the next annihilated by the night.

The Engineer stood for a minute, as though he was going to head off to his tent. But instead, he slowly unbuttoned his sou'wester, exposing his white shirt tucked into the black officer's pants. He pulled the front of his shirt out of his pants and held it up to his chin, baring his midriff. There, just above the waistline, the watchers could all see a long horizontal scar, a white corrugation about nine inches long dissecting his pale, northern skin.

The men were silent. The Engineer carefully tucked his shirt back into his trousers, pulled his sou'wester together, turned and walked away into the darkness.

6

Daniel Stevenson, my grandfather, had almost finished his story. In the dull light of the attic, his yellow-green eyes were growing old again, as the elapsed thirty years filled back in.

'The next day, I asked the Engineer what were the names of the children. He said they all had biblical names: his sisters were called Rachel and Esther, his brother, Amos. And himself, Zachary. He said he was glad I asked.'

Daniel Stevenson was lying back as he told me this, his lips barely moving, so that his head might have been a skull, with an army of tiny, stale-smelling black ants crawling over his jaw-bone, their legs rustling out the sounds, 'Rachel,' 'Esther,' 'Amos,' 'Zachary.' He lay exhausted, as though something vital had been cut out of him. Throughout the entire story, his hoarse voice had been, at times, scarcely more than a whisper that conspired with the swish of the rain on the grey slates of the attic roof to make sure no one else in the world could hear, but me, Ezra Stevenson.

7

As I said, I only knew Daniel Stevenson, my grandfather, for a week. He had run away from Muirton, our village high in the moors, thirty years before. On a gloomy September morning, he had been walking along the hawthorn-hedge-lined roadway to the mine, for the early shift, with five other men. The time was just before six-thirty in the morning. As they passed the red-brick railway station, the weekly passenger train was about to leave for the coast. Daniel Stevenson, who was not dressed for travelling, quietly said goodbye to his workmates, vaulted over the station's picket fence, and hauled himself aboard the train, which was already moving. He left behind him, in Muirton, a wife and a young son.

Then, thirty years later, he came home.

Once again, it was September, but the weather was cold and windy. In Muirton, winter was often hard to tell from summer, for the temperature did not vary much up in the moorland hills. But at a certain time in September, the leaves of the few trees that grew there would cast off and tack wearily to their final berths.

In September, then, Daniel Stevenson came home. Really home, that is. He moved right into our house without anyone noticing he was back. He must have come in during the night, for doors were seldom locked in villages like Muirton, where burglary was much less common than those crimes locked doors only encouraged.

Daniel Stevenson must have entered by the back door, slunk across the brown linoleum floor of the kitchen (he would have noticed the smell of floor-polish and cooking) to the brown-painted door of the attic stairway, then climbed the narrow, enclosed stairs that sneaked up along the side wall of the house to the attic, once a maid's quarters. And settled down.

How he even knew which house was ours is a mystery. His grown-up son, John Stevenson (my father: a man who never sang, who had never been known to join, even, in communal singing), had become the manager of the mine just three years before. Only then had we moved from the small row-house, among all the other miners' rows, into this big house, formerly the mine-owner's mansion, at the edge of the village.

How did the old man know we lived there now? Had he been spying on us for a while before he entered? Not very likely. In that village, a stranger would have been too obvious. And, anyway, how would he have known what his wife and son looked like after thirty years? Unless someone else was collaborating with him? Someone who never owned up, not even afterwards? Perhaps. These things cannot now be determined. What is sure is that one night he must have come up into the kitchen through the back door, put on his old carpet slippers (a point, surely, worthy of note), and climbed up into that attic cautiously. Caution was needed, for the stairs passed a part of the wall of the main bedroom. The Stevenson house was a house of light sleepers.

8

The woman who was my grandmother, Joanna Stevenson, was the first to notice he was back. She was of middle size, with grey eyes, fine features (though her nose wandered off slightly to her left), her hair held back by a wooden clasp carved in the shape of entwined snakes. In the centre of her long grey hair was a thick, black streak that had not aged.

She was the one who saw that the worn felt slippers she had preserved for thirty years had disappeared from the boot-tray by the back door. She was the one who found out that bread and cheese and apples and milk were missing from the pantry. She knew this with certainty, for it was her pantry, she was in charge of the kitchen.

She said nothing.

Once or twice during the early days of the return, my mother, Elizabeth Stevenson, thought she heard a faint creaking of boards in the attic. She was soft faced and plump, characteristics of many of the women in Muirton. But she was a fiery woman, orphaned as a child. So when she heard something up there, she urged John Stevenson to take a piece of wood, and go up and kill whatever creature was making the noise, for it might be a mouse or, even worse, a rat. She said, as she frequently did, how foolish it was not to kill those things that ought to be killed. She was in charge of keeping the house clean.

John Stevenson, my father, was a red-haired man

(red hair was another common Muirton trait), heavy shouldered from mine work, a man who ordered other men about all day, but who was happy at home to submit to Elizabeth. Unless my grandmother, Joanna, contradicted her, as she did now. She said the noise wasn't mice or rats at this time of year, just the wind. Elizabeth looked at her and looked at her, a long time.

9

In those days, Joanna began to change her behaviour. She had always gone to bed early, even before me, and I was only ten at that time. But now, she would stay up after the rest of us, saying she wanted to do some reading (something I had never, in my ten years, seen her do) or knitting. Or just sit there by the night fire a little longer.

What she'd really do, after we had all said good-night and gone to our rooms and fallen asleep, was this: she'd take the old Golden Jubilee tin tray down from the sideboard and load it with buttered bread, and perhaps a piece of beef, a bottle of stout, and some rhubarb pie. She'd leave the tray on the deal table in the kitchen with a clean shirt and fresh woollen socks. Then she'd go up to bed.

In the night, Daniel Stevenson, the unacknowledged

guest, would slip down, take the tray and the clothes, and creep back up to the attic.

Night after night, she prepared food and clothing for him in this way. Night after night, he came down the stairs to return the dirty things and pick up his provisions. She would get up first in the mornings, despite her late nights, to clear away the evidence.

So he knew, of course, that she knew he was back.

10

But one morning (I suppose he had been in the attic at least two weeks) when she got up, the tray and the clothing still lay untouched on the deal table. All day, she wondered what was wrong. That night, she set the provisions out for him again. She went to bed, but was hardly able to sleep for worrying. Was he lying up there, sick or dead? Had he, perhaps, finished whatever it was he had come home to do, and had left Muirton again, without her knowing? She could not bear that thought. She got up just before dawn, went down to the kitchen, and saw the fresh clothes and food still lying on the table. That was enough.

She went straight to the main bedroom, which she had never before entered, opened the door and walked in. My parents, John and Elizabeth Stevenson, had, of course, heard her, and were in the act of sitting up with the blankets half-around them, like creatures to whom a lumpy monster was giving birth.

What must have passed through their heads as that old woman told them what had been going on for two weeks in their house? How she wanted her son to go right up to the attic and see if Daniel was all right. How she was afraid he was dead, or that he'd gone away again.

John Stevenson, whatever he might have thought, heaved himself into the cold air of the bedroom and went down (a descent in order to ascend) to the brightly lit kitchen, opened the attic stairway door and, taking a broom-handle with him, just in case, began climbing the narrow staircase into the attic. His wife and his mother stayed in the kitchen.

11

When John Stevenson came down from the attic, hours later, he did not tell the women what it felt like to meet his father after all those years. He was not one to speak about his feelings. He tried, instead, to tell them what he had heard. It is difficult enough for any man to match his supply of words, most of them worn smooth and round, like stones in a river, with the erratic, jagged truths of experience. John Stevenson, a man of few words, could only give an outline of what Daniel Stevenson had told him about his thirty years' absence. Here is what he said.

Daniel, after he had run away, travelled from country to country working at any job a strong back qualified him for: bricklayer, longshoreman, sailor. Mainly sailor. A travelling life. The last ten years, however, he had spent living on the island of Oluba, in the South Pacific Ocean. The island had been a port of call when he worked on the copra schooners. He had a woman there, and a family of Stevensons, too.

A year ago, he found out he was dying, and for the first time in thirty years, he wanted to come home. He was not afraid of death, but he wanted to be near them all: his wife, his son, his daughter-in-law, if there was one, his grandchildren, if there were any (I, Ezra, was the only one). He wanted to die in the place where he was born, to exchange hibiscus for heather.

As for Oluba and his life there, the Olubans did not like the idea of a foreigner dying amongst them. They were fearful his spirit (they believed in such things) might never settle. He had always known he'd have to leave. He agreed with the Olubans that life was a journey, and it was right for a man to close out his travels in his own home port, in the place where he had begun them.

Now, up there in the attic, he would not hear of allowing a doctor near him. That was not, he said, why he came home. He assured John Stevenson he had seen men die, and knew how to die. His dying would give them no trouble.

'Syphilis, most likely,' was Elizabeth's comment on it all.

Joanna Stevenson, who had listened with great attention to the life story of the old man, her husband, was silent. In her eyes and on her face were traces of what might have been a smile.

12

He stayed alive for another week. He said he did not wish to see anyone but his son, John. Joanna continued to prepare his food (Elizabeth would have nothing to do with him: 'Wasn't I right? A rat in the attic?'). He wouldn't see any of his former workmates, either, though word was all round the village that he was back, and some of the old men would have liked to talk to him. According to John, Daniel Stevenson said he hadn't come back to talk to people, he wanted to remember them the way they had been. He wouldn't even look out of the windows in daylight in case Muirton had changed. He would only talk to his son, who took care of the old man's physical needs, helping him eat, change his shirt, support him to the grimy attic toilet, unused since the last maid lived there many years ago.

13

This is where I come into it.

At the beginning of that week, the last week of Daniel Stevenson's life, on a wet Monday afternoon, when rain obscured the hills and the smell of coal smoke was in the air, he changed his mind about not talking to anyone and said he did want to talk to his grandson. (That's me, Ezra.) I don't know why I wasn't at school that day. Maybe I had pretended illness, I often did that. John Stevenson, my father, came down from the attic with the request. When Elizabeth heard it, she was against my going up. Joanna Stevenson, my grandmother, stayed silent, and I couldn't tell from her face what she thought.

I do remember being afraid of going up there. Not because I knew I would have to meet an old man who was not like the other old men of Muirton. No, the real reason was that even though I was only ten, or because I was only ten, I sensed that everything was about to become too complicated. Since the discovery of Daniel Stevenson's return, the atmosphere in the house had not been the same. In the past, we had never, as a family, talked much. We did the things families do, but we didn't talk about them. Now, with him upstairs in the attic, family conversation was even scarcer. My grandmother Joanna's body seemed to me to be inhabited by an unknown person who had grey eyes that were too bright, and whose lips were constantly rehearsing a faint, unfamiliar smile.

I agreed, nonetheless, to go up to the attic.

14

I glued my hand to the great, red-bristled hand of my father, and we climbed the steep stairs to the attic, a place I had been in only once and feared, because of the mottled light, the gritty floor, the cobwebs, the real vermin, the imaginary bats, the ghosts of ancient housemaids under shrouded furniture, the bent rolls of carpet, like broken cigarettes, the smell of decay, of sadness. I could not help feeling, as we climbed, that a gloomy monster was slowly devouring us. Its insides stank of urine and sour breath.

15

The old felt slippers are on the floor near the mattress where the old man lies, on his side, under the bare bulb. Weather and age have clawed the flesh around his yellow-green eyes that aim out from under a battlement of thick grey eyebrows. Half his body protrudes from the shell of blankets as he beckons feebly, a snail waving its antennae.

The boy uses his father's hip as a shield. Thinking this sick old man with the yellow skin, this man who smells so sick, is his grandfather. The face is a mask of fine wrinkles, hiding the man beneath. This old man looks like a painting in a book, symbolizing something.

As he raises himself on an elbow, the seamed yellow of his stomach shows through the placket of his shirt. The hands squeezed out by the white shirt-sleeves are yellow too, the fingers are still a miner's blunt fingers, but without the crescents of coal-dust.

The green-yellow, yellow-green eyes examine the boy. The remnants of the life that is retreating from his body have gathered in the circles of his eyes.

'So, Ezra. It's good to meet you.'

Such an adult greeting to a ten-year-old boy. His voice is brittle by the time it reaches his lips. The accent is almost foreign, that of a man who has for too many years eaten strange foods.

16

In that final week of his life, I spent hour after hour listening to him talking, talking. In his brittle, urgent voice, he spoke about things he had done and places he had been since he had left Muirton thirty years before. He'd visited the most remote parts of the world, and he loved to tell me about them ('Did you ever hear of Oluba?' he'd begin; or 'Did you ever hear of the River Merape?'; or 'Did you ever hear of Cape Horn?'). He'd seen animals and men of every description, and he'd faced danger and death.

Always, when I came downstairs after these sessions, Joanna, my grandmother, would be waiting. I would tell her all the old man had said, and she would listen with great attention, asking me for details (especially when he told me about the women he'd encountered on his journeys, his eyes shining with pleasure as he talked). I would try to memorize the important words and transmit them to her. She would listen with that look in her grey eyes, that movement of the lips that never quite became a smile. He knew I told her everything, and when next I went to visit him, he would ask me if she had made any comment on his adventures.

In all those long conversations, he never wanted to know anything else about her. How strange that seems to me now. But no more strange than that a boy of ten could have enjoyed so much the role of go-between, observer.

17

It was on one of those afternoons that he told me about his journey to Patagonia, and the story of Zachary Mackenzie and his sisters and brother. I remember, afterwards, going downstairs. Joanna was waiting for me in the kitchen. I could smell the freshly made tea, as usual.

'Well?'

She waited for me to talk. But I said I didn't feel like tea or talk, I wanted to go outside. I put on my coat, trying not to look at her, and went outside into the cold air. And even though I told her nothing, I felt I had lied to her for the first time in my life, and I was sure she knew it. I don't know why I didn't, but I didn't tell her the story that day, or any other day, no matter how she looked at me from then on.

18

The last Sunday morning was a dreary one, rain and fog mixed. We ate breakfast silently, and when I had finished John Stevenson told me to run up to the attic, and see how the old man was, for he hadn't been too well earlier.

As I entered the attic, a little breathless, Daniel Stevenson didn't turn his head to greet me. I went over to the mattress and looked down at him. His face was as grim as the morning. He lay flat, staring at the peaked attic ceiling. The yellow-green eyes were very yellow, and no longer shining.

He took a noisy, shallow breath, and whispered: 'Ezra. Get your grandmother.'

I ran back down the narrow stairs into the kitchen where the three of them were sitting finishing off their bacon and eggs. The fire was blazing. Their faces, even John Stevenson's now, even Elizabeth's, all of them were like strangers' as they turned to look at me. Perhaps I knew what was going to happen, perhaps not. That day was so long ago, and so many things to understand. But I was excited by the strangeness of their faces.

'He wants you,' I said to my grandmother, Joanna Stevenson.

Did I hope, even then, that she would go rushing up to him? I like to think so. She smiled at me, not that trace of smile I had seen her lips nurture for many days, but the fully developed version of it, an unpleasant smile.

The three of them sat there, without moving. So I said, again, just to make sure: 'He wants you.'

It was John, my father, who spoke.

'Ezra, you go outside and play till dinner-time.'

I was about to protest. What about the rain? What about the old man up there? Instead, I went slowly to the back door, and took my raincoat from its hook. I kept glancing to the right, towards the open door to the attic stairway, listening for any sound. Was that his voice, a very weak voice calling her name? Or my name? Didn't he understand yet? I looked back to the table where the three of them sat, watching me.

They must have seen, at that moment, the last flicker of boyhood in that boy of ten's eyes, the painful recognition that the world could no longer be, never really had been, his own invention.

19

I stepped outside, pulling the back door closed behind me quickly, so that I would hear no more, and I walked away up towards the hills.

The air smelt cold and hard after the warmth inside. I made my way from the house, from the village, across narrow fields and fat, opaque streams, till the land began to rise much more steeply. The rain was pouring now, on my bare head. I climbed and climbed, leaning hard into the hill, the wet bracken soaking me to the waist. At times the gusts of wind were slabs of stone.

After about two hours, I stopped and looked back for the first time. I was perhaps a thousand feet above the village. Muirton huddled in a crack of valley, the smoke belching from a thousand chimneys. The buildings lay like broken letters of an alphabet, the remnants of their message half obliterated by the rain. All around, the noose of blunt hills seemed tighter than usual, and I could see no way out, except far to the west, where they dipped a little towards the coastal plain.

Something came over me then. I may have wept, but my face was already wet from the pouring rain, so that no one in the universe could have known for sure if I was crying. And if I cried, the tears must have been saved up for many years, and it was a long time before I began to make my way down to the village.

20

When I returned to the house, it was almost dark. Elizabeth, my mother, was in the kitchen slicing onions for dinner. She said Joanna and John Stevenson were up in the attic, and that she herself would join them in a while. I asked if I should go up, and she said: 'Yes, for a minute.'

In the attic, the two of them were standing by the mattress, holding hands. The old slippers still lay on the floor. My grandmother, Joanna Stevenson, turned to me as I came in and told me what I already knew.

'He's dead.'

She spoke again, smiling that way: 'He died up here, alone.'

I tried to keep all expression out of my face. He was stretched out on the mattress, looking the way he always did, except for the dead eyes.

We heard the heavy creak of the stairs. Elizabeth, my mother. She came into the attic, slightly out of breath, and went straight to grandmother Joanna Stevenson. For the first time in my life I saw her embrace Joanna, her plump right hand stroking the back of my grandmother's head, her fingers touching the wooden fastener with the entwined snakes that held the grey hair and the black streak neatly apart. She kissed her cheek. Only then did she glance down at the dead man.

'So that was him,' she said.

We were all looking down at the corpse of the old man, and I couldn't get it out of my head that the four of us, Joanna Stevenson, Elizabeth Stevenson, John Stevenson, and myself, Ezra Stevenson, even though we were on our feet and breathing, were no more alive than he was. It was an awful feeling. But I was young enough, then, to be certain that it would go away.

'Come down now, Ezra,' said Elizabeth Stevenson, my mother.

Then she took me firmly by the hand and led me downstairs, and I remember that my hand was moist, but hers was dry as sand.

21

Nothing more needs to be said about my grandfather, Daniel Stevenson. He served his purpose. Whatever kind of man he was, he brought the Mackenzie story out of Patagonia, handed it on to me in Muirton, and died.

And that was that.

As for Muirton itself, it died too, not long after the old man's death (Elizabeth Stevenson, my mother, saw a direct link between the one thing and the other, a cause and effect).

Early on a July morning, forty Muirton miners, men and boys, were in the cage, descending the mine-shaft to the coal-face, when the cable snapped. The cage plunged, uncontrolled, one thousand metres down the shaft. When it struck bottom, twenty-seven of the miners died outright, and thirteen were maimed. That maiming was the cause of an unwanted, fleeting celebrity for Muirton: it became known as the village of the one-legged men.

Every single one of those who survived the disaster lost a leg. The miners had followed the safety procedures they'd practised since their apprenticeships: when they saw that the cage was plummeting out of control, they reached up and grasped the leather straps attached to the struts of the ceiling for just such a situation, then each of them lifted one of his legs off the floor. As the cage slammed into the bottom of the mine-shaft, the straps snapped, the legs that supported their body-weight were smashed to a pulp, but their lives were saved.

For years after, people from the capital used to take their Sunday drives to Muirton in the hope of spotting one of the survivors. What would have been regarded as a tragedy, had it happened to only one man, was transformed into a farce because of the number of the survivors and the bizarre nature of the injury.

But the people of Muirton fooled the sightseers. While the injured men became adept at disguising their limps, many of the uninjured villagers, men and women, cultivated an exaggerated hobbling walk. Almost all of the children of Muirton learnt to limp expertly. Who knows what the visitors made of it all?

The disaster caused the permanent closing of the mine, which had not been very profitable. A few years later, the village itself was deserted. Even the one-legged men went their separate ways to other mining towns, where their uniqueness enabled them to find some dignity, if not anonymity, once more.

And what about the other Stevensons? They're all dead now. Joanna died a year after Daniel, having no reason to wait any more. John Stevenson, my father, was kept on as superintendent of the derelict mine property, to check the gas levels and monitor ground shifts in those endless dark excisions of the earth's core. He and my mother, Elizabeth, lived out the remainder of their lives in Muirton, the ghost town, and died in due course, in the old run-down house.

As for me, Ezra Stevenson (I had noticed, even as a boy, the curious fact that my name, E-Z-R-A, was an acronym for the names of those four Mackenzies: E-sther,

Z-achary, R-achel, A-mos), though my own story is of little importance, I may as well dispose of it here, in the interest of neatness. I went through the educational grind, without distinction (no matter how many books I read, wisdom eluded me), and eventually graduated after a university career memorable only for friendships with one or two fine women, and with Donald Cromarty. He was a student of the more obscure regions of sixteenth-century history. And he was a careful, honest man. He *will* have a conclusive role in all of this, later, at the Paradise Motel.

A couple of years after graduation, I set out, like thousands of others, for the New World. I stayed for a while. I thought it might be possible to live contented here, and so I stayed longer. I have lived half my life here now. I travel a lot, I meet people. And I have a good friend, Helen.

22

Did I say nothing more needed to be said about my grandfather, Daniel Stevenson? I take that back, for a moment, just to tell one last thing.

I heard about it on the day of his funeral. (I would have preferred to avoid talking about funerals. But so much of this happened so long ago, and so many people are dead. The past often seems like one of those cornfields in the autumn, when the stalks are left standing, to wither.)

The day was an unpleasant one. Muirton could be relied on for good funeral weather. The rain was even heavier than usual. The church, with its panoply of spiky gravestones, was a fortress against joy. On that day, its blunt forefinger of a steeple warned the heavens against any such unwanted frivolity as a glimpse of sun. Hardly anyone attended the service, for it was a weekday, and most of the men were at work in the mine.

After the damp silence of the church, the graveyard was noisy with the splat of rain on umbrellas, on the muddy ground, and on the heavy wooden coffin. John Stevenson and I, four local men who helped carry the coffin, two grave-diggers, and the clergyman were the only witnesses. After the ornate coffin was lowered into the fresh-smelling earth, I threw in a piece of mud. The clunk of it against the darkly varnished wood was satisfying.

My father and I, chilled and hungry, walked back to the big house after the burial. The two women were in the kitchen, waiting. As we warmed ourselves by the fire, I asked my grandmother, Joanna, the question that was foremost in my mind: would she give me the contents of Grandfather Daniel Stevenson's pockets, especially the scrimshawed ship? Smiling faintly, she shook her head. She'd burnt everything, she said, everything of his was gone up in smoke.

John Stevenson, to change the subject, told the two of them how the clergyman had said a few words at the graveside to the effect that it was good for a grandchild to have known his own grandfather, even if only for a week. How we should be thankful that, in the end, the prodigal had come home after his long journey.

Elizabeth couldn't restrain herself.

'Long journey? What long journey? Rubbish!' she said.

She'd heard another version of Daniel Stevenson's life several times in the past few days. Even that very morning, while we were at the funeral, when she'd gone to shop for groceries, the storekeeper told her the rumour was all round the village. That Daniel Stevenson *didn't* go very far the morning he'd run away, thirty years ago. What he really did was this: he stayed on the train till it came to one of those little mining towns, Lannock, only thirty miles away to the south. Lannock was a replica of Muirton, as were most of those small mining towns in the hills. They all had their heaps of slag, their coal smoke, and rain. Daniel got off the train at Lannock, found a room to rent, and within a week, started work in the mine there. He had worked there, all those years, living on his own, till he became ill and returned to Muirton.

'Long journey! He didn't go anywhere!' Elizabeth said.

John Stevenson grunted. It was always hard to know what he really thought, he was such a quiet man. My grandmother, Joanna, looked as though she'd heard the story from Elizabeth already, and anyway, was no longer interested; just that faint smile whenever anyone mentioned Daniel Stevenson.

I didn't say a thing, because at my age, what could I

say? At that time, for me, the barrier between truth and a convincing story was so fragile that I could penetrate it with ease, from either side. I did not see the need, in the interest of coherence in the world, for the segregation of the two.

23

That funeral was many years ago. I was remembering it and the events that led up to it, on a recent summer morning, on the balcony of my third-floor apartment. Helen was carrying out the coffee-pot to pour another cup, stepping carefully (I always pretended not to notice) to avoid the flowers on the living-room carpet. Just then, as she refilled my cup, I was remembering that boy Ezra, still inside me somewhere, but overgrown by this middle-aged, grey-haired Ezra; the one who lived in an expensive apartment overlooking the lake in the park, in a country where breakfast on the balcony in summer was possible; the one who could take a trip, at a whim, to the east coast and the Paradise Motel; the one who lived with a woman of satisfying beauty and wit, a wisp of whose fair hair had been in his mouth that morning when he awoke. To whom he occasionally liked to tell, as a variety of love-making, bits and pieces of his early life, so remote it might have been someone else's.

On that warm summer morning, as the smell of cut grass from the park drifted in with the scent of the coffee, I began telling Helen, now sitting opposite me, about Daniel Stevenson, and how he passed Zachary Mackenzie's story on to me. I told her that I had always regarded it as my personal inheritance from the old man, and how, when I was about sixteen and going through a poetic phase, I sometimes thought of the story in a romantic way, as some force inside Daniel Stevenson that had kept him alive all those years. He had begun to die so soon after passing it on to me.

I said that as I grew older I wondered if the story wasn't more of a poison he had swallowed, a rotting thing within him that brought him, at last, to his grave. Maybe he had got rid of it too late. I believed then, and still do, that even a thing made of words can grow inside the body, like gallstones which will one day make their necessary and painful exit.

I told Helen that I came to consider the story, years later, as nothing more than a story told to an impressionable boy, who eventually grew up to be too sophisticated to take it literally. It was nothing but the baggage of dreams. And yet I had kept it to myself.

Till now. Now, I wanted Helen to hear it. I wondered what she would think, for she was very astute. Like her father, a man who could make fishing lures, flies that were so genuine the fish did not notice the tiny hooks under their perfect wings. I wanted to tell her Zachary

Mackenzie's story as I had heard it from my grandfather, so that it would affect her the way it had affected me when I was a boy.

But words seem to have the quality of magnets that, in time, become so smothered in pins, and scraps of this and that, they have no force left. As I spoke, the old words were no longer spare and correct, the way they had once seemed to me. I could hardly stop myself from smiling, as I told her about the burial of the limbs inside the children, and about the scar on Zachary Mackenzie's belly. The whole thing sounded so improbable, I even told Helen that, in retrospect, the rumour was probably true that Daniel Stevenson hadn't travelled at all, that he hadn't escaped, only wished it all, a pathetic old man.

Helen smiled while I told her this, but her blue eyes, behind their peculiar, convex lower lids, were not smiling.

And when she saw I was finished, she asked: 'What happened to them all?'

'What do you mean?'

'The three children. Rachel, Amos, and Esther. Or Zachary, after your grandfather met him? Did he ever say what happened to any of them?'

'No. You think Daniel did go to Patagonia? You think the Mackenzies actually existed? Do you really?'

'Well, I don't know. Maybe.'

She looked at me, or perhaps through me.

'But maybe it's better not to know. Maybe it's better just to forget the whole thing.'

24

That afternoon, more for the fun of it than anything else, a silly thing to do, really, I wrote a letter to my old scholarly friend, Donald Cromarty, who was now Professor Donald Cromarty. It was a long letter. I told him everything: about Muirton, and Daniel Stevenson, and the *Mingulay*, and the expedition to Patagonia, and the Mackenzies. I asked him (I knew he wouldn't mind; this was exactly the kind of thing he loved to do) if there was any way he could find out, at his leisure, whether there was any substance to the story. I asked him to do it for Helen's sake (though I did not tell Helen I was writing to him). I assured him I, personally, thought it was all nonsense. But I said I'd be grateful to him, nonetheless.

And that night, as Helen and I lay in bed, looking out through the picture window at the stars arranging themselves into wild beasts, she said that my reluctance about telling the Patagonian story till now was more revealing than anything else she'd ever discovered about me.

I think she may have been right. Odd isn't it? How you know it within yourself that what you *don't* say is so important. How almost everything you *do* say is just camouflage, or perhaps armour, or perhaps the bandage over the wound.

Part Two

AMOS

At the age of eight Amos Mackenzie was consigned to 'The Abbey,' a home for waifs and strays (boys only), in the south of England. The institute was operated by the priests of the Holy Order of Correction. For five years he was the victim of a debilitating stutter, which caused him to drag himself from one consonant to the next, like a climber scaling a difficult rock-face. On the day of his thirteenth birthday, the stutter disappeared. By then, he had grown into a lean, ugly boy.

Botany was the only academic subject in which he expressed interest. In class, he often shocked his priest-instructors with his comparisons, suggesting once, for example, that the undersurfaces of certain leaves were 'as soft as the inside of a girl's thigh.' He said this without guile, so the teacher did not dare reprimand him. The boy had an intensity about him that disconcerted all prospective bullies.

At the beginning of his fourteenth year, he left the orphanage and found a job in the Botanical Gardens. He secretly believed that human society was little different from a collection of plants distinguished by sex, skin, smell, and colour, and flourishing in a variety of climates; and that if only a method could be worked out for determining which were the flowers, which the weeds, the blights of war and disease would be eliminated. The human practice of burying the dead was, for him, a wasteful perversion of the idea of planting seeds. Dead humans, he felt, ought either to be burnt, the way any good gardener burns off the residues at the end of the growing season; or they ought to be heaped into containers and allowed to turn into a mulch, for fertilizing new plants in the spring of the year. His daily exercise in those days was to walk round the park near his lodgings, and admire the 'natural families' there. By which he meant the pairs of adult trees with their seedlings around them.

In the years after he left the orphanage, he met his brothers and the rest of his family only once. As he grew older, his youthful ugliness remained; that, together with a voice harsher than a winter wind, imparted a crudeness to what he said, no matter how elegant his language. He was never known to smile or make jokes. He never formed an attachment to any woman, but carried in his pocket a collection of female seeds which he would fondle gently from time to time.

Then, around the age of forty-five, he developed quite suddenly a passion for anthropology and archaeology. It was the idea of probing the roots of human culture and of unearthing lost artefacts that exhilarated him. His unprepossessing face became almost beautiful as he imagined how it must feel to take a machete (he liked the idea of a machete) to the brittle shell of appearances, and liberate raw truth with one blow.

He had found his vocation.

Notebook, A. McGAW

1

That year, early in August, I said my goodbyes to Helen and went down to the South Pacific to visit the Institute for the Lost, a research establishment situated on an island thirty miles offshore in the Coral Sea. The quickest way to get there was by plane from the mainland. We flew out over the coastline, and, from five thousand feet, I saw the island, a crescent-shaped scar on the smooth belly of the ocean. Our seaplane swooped down and landed on the lagoon.

Around the Institute itself, lawns of tough tropical grass were engaged in futile battles with the invading sand, while palm trees tried to hold their ground against the persistent, sour-smelling trade wind. The Institute consisted of two large L-shaped buildings, with some flimsy bungalows at the tops of the L's, all of them bracketing a blue-tiled swimming pool that looked as though it was never used. It was a tiny inland sea of dead leaves and live lizards.

A small woman, quite stooped, came down the steps of the main building into the sun (it was always summer there) to meet me. I recognized her from photographs: Doctor Yerdeli, the Director. From close up, I could see how lined her cheeks were and how, when she spoke, her mouth had a foreign twist. Her white hair was very white, and her lab coat was spotless, but the stethoscope that dangled like a divining rod round her neck and over her chest had metal ends with scabs of rust. As she welcomed me, she gesticulated with her left hand, as though she was conducting a piece of music, slow music, for she was a deliberate speaker. Whenever her sleeve fell back during one of these gestures, I could not help noticing the series of numbers tatooed in blue ink just above her wrist.

In spite of her formality, in spite of her stoop, she seemed pleased to see me. I had requested an interview with her some months before, for I had thought she might be able to help me with a biography I was researching at that time (the life of a well-known, now dead philanthropist who had spent years in that region). In her reply, she had said that she could be of no help, but that I might find her own work here interesting.

So here I was, and here she stood. At times, as she spoke in her slow way, she would squint her eyes upward, into her skull, reminding me of someone reciting a speech learnt by heart or else translating words written in another language on some mental pad. This quirk caused an emptiness between her words. As we were going inside for a tour of the main building, she said:

'We have so many visitors. But sometimes they can be utterly . . . delightful.' I had feared she was searching for a less flattering word. She said, too, that publicity was always good for the Institute and brought interesting cases, as well as wealthy visitors from all round the world.

'I'm afraid I don't fit either category,' I said.

'Your certainty is . . . admirable,' she said, in her hesitant way. Then laughed a surprisingly quick, light laugh.

In the corridor of that first building, a brisk-looking man wearing the same white coat and rusty stethoscope as Doctor Yerdeli was walking in our direction. The man, whose eyes seemed to me particularly alert, must have presumed that, since I was with the Director, I was a medical man, for he greeted us both in a formal manner as 'Doctor.' I was about to correct him, to let him know I was no doctor. But Doctor Yerdeli took my arm and urged me on along the corridor. When we were out of his hearing range, she told me that it was just as well to let him believe whatever he liked, for the man was here for treatment and might become disoriented by any challenges. Playing roles was often the prescription for certain cases, so playing at being a doctor might well be an important part of his treatment.

'And of my treatment too, of course,' she said. And laughed in that quick way.

2

As we walked along, she opened doors here and there, and showed me some of the Institute's offices, its comfortable lounges, its cafeteria, the research lab with its whiff of ether, the insulated counselling rooms. The Institute, she told me, specialized in the treatment of amnesia. She welcomed three basic types of students (the word 'patient' was anathema to her). The first were those who were delivered to her in a chronic amnesiac state caused by some accident; their original identities were irrecoverable. The second were those who could no longer bear themselves and who, in spite of years of therapy, insisted on having substitute identities; some of these students had even, by a deliberate act of the will, erased their memories. The third were made up of a variety of students, not necessarily amnesiacs, who for any reason excited Doctor Yerdeli's curiosity; they were known as 'The Director's Specials,' and she worked personally with them.

The Institute could only deal with up to ten students at a time, though dozens applied for admission each month. Aside from her work with her 'Specials,' Doctor Yerdeli's main occupation, and that of her colleagues (whom I saw briefly, from time to time), was to invent new lives and pasts for her students.

I interrupted her: 'Do any of them ever reject the new lives you make up for them?'

She did not answer this immediately, so I rephrased my question:

'You spoke of those who come to you knowingly for substitute identities. Are the lives you make up for them always more satisfying than the ones they rejected before?'

She assured me she was not avoiding giving an answer. It was just that she wanted to think first. Smiling a little, she said she could speak for all of her colleagues in saying that their profession was totally satisfying. Indeed it was an art rather than a science. Simply put, she had to create for each student in her care a story with a main persona (a favourite term of hers), a stock of subsidiary figures, all of them developed enough to be credible, and a vast array of appropriate facts. Then she had to coach her student to *be*, convincingly, the new persona, no matter how long it might take.

I was about to interrupt again, but she held up a hand. She was working her way round to answering my question.

Granted, she said, as with any artist, sometimes a sketch would turn out badly, a character might have to be excised, no matter how painful that might be to the creator. But the method itself was sound. Years ago, after a few such disappointments, she had thought it better to use already created characters from novels as personae for her students. That had been a failure. Literary characters seemed to violate credibility in some way that made them useless, even dangerous. Such classical creations as Becky Sharp, or Horatio Hornblower, or Molly Bloom, or Agent 007 (she had used them all at one time or another) turned out to be flimsy verbal scaffoldings that collapsed in the sweat and stress of life, when the actual people around them no longer adhered to a pre-determined plot. She wished that some of the literary critics who lauded these fictional characters had been able to see how poorly they fared in real life!

Another danger of this method was that, in spite of

all her warnings, the students to whom characters from literature were allocated would secretly read the novels in which their prototypes appeared, and try to emulate them. The results were predictable and disastrous. She had resolved to write a paper on the hazards of the practice, she said, smiling again.

'These matters are so . . . complex.'

I understood that this was all of the answer she intended to give to my question, so I left it at that.

3

In the course of this preliminary stroll around the Institute, I was surprised at how often Doctor Yerdeli returned to the question of her image. At times, she said she thought of herself as a plastic surgeon of the mind, cutting away residual rot, and reshaping what was left. But she much preferred the view of herself as an artist. Yes, she said, she was more a sculptor of the psyche than anything else.

One thing I could see plainly: in spite of her frail appearance, she was enthusiastic about her work, and seemed to be a kind woman. Her students either needed or wanted a new persona, and all she asked from them in return was that they present her with what she liked to call a *tabula rasa*, a blank slate on which she would delineate her attempted masterpieces.

At one point, I remember asking her:

'Have you or any of your colleagues ever invented characters that exceed you? That are, say, wiser than you yourselves are?'

Again, I thought for a moment she was going to ignore my question. But eventually, in that deliberate manner, as though she was reading from an already prepared script, she said:

'My colleagues are too ... intelligent to do such a thing.' She laughed her quick laugh.

4

Doctor Yerdeli was sure I would like to meet one or two of her students. She took me outside to where one of them, a tall, middle-aged woman with faded dress and faded brown hair, sat on a lawn-chair, frowning into the morass that was the swimming pool.

The woman glanced up nervously at us, then went back to her scrutiny of lizards and leaves. Doctor Yerdeli put a hand comfortingly on her shoulder and began to tell me about her; or perhaps I should say, deliver a prepared lecture to me; she seemed to have lost her hesitations.

'This is Maria. Authorities in the south sent her to us. She suffered a total loss of memory after being knocked down by a car. She was carrying no identification, except for a bracelet with the name "Maria" on it. No amount of advertising could find anyone who knew her. She wasted two years in a hospital down there before they sent her here.'

Maria seemed to be paying no attention to us as Doctor Yerdeli spoke. I presumed the students were quite accustomed to such demonstrations. Indeed, I wondered if this public narration was for my benefit or for Maria's, or whether Doctor Yerdeli was simply enjoying an opportunity to display her art, smiling as she talked.

Maria, it seems, settled into the Institute, and showed herself to be co-operative and intelligent. Doctor Yerdeli immediately began to invent a new persona for her. She decided, after studying Maria for a while, to give her a cautious character: she would make Maria a spinster schoolteacher from any one of a thousand little outback towns where everybody knows everybody else. She would make her a specialist in history, a soprano in the church choir (why not?), a well-adjusted woman content with small-town life. Just to give her existence some tinge of pathos and adventure (I could see Doctor Yerdeli relished this part of her creation), Maria would have a secret memory of a sexual interlude in her early twenties and a back-street abortion.

Doctor Yerdeli invented hundreds of such details, spending countless hours elaborating on them, drilling

Maria in them daily. Until Maria herself became persuaded of the possibilities and entered into the spirit of the persona, manufacturing details on her own, filling in the gaps. She was beginning to make it her own invention, she was on her way to believing that this was, indeed, her life.

Then, just when she was settling into her new persona, starting to feel whole again, a peculiar thing happened. One morning, she came rushing into Doctor Yerdeli's office, babbling excitedly: she remembered everything! She remembered who she really was! During the night, her own, original memory had come back to her!

Doctor Yerdeli calmed her, made her sit down and talk.

Maria repeated that it had all come back to her. She really had been a schoolteacher from a small town in the bush. She congratulated Doctor Yerdeli on her perceptiveness. She remembered the name of the town she lived in, it was called Kikiburee. She did indeed have a degree, but in geography, not history; and though she was in the church choir at Kikiburee, St Martin's Church, she was actually a contralto.

As Maria talked, Doctor Yerdeli was sure she was simply embellishing some of the details of her new persona to her own taste. She was convinced Maria was displaying the symptoms of a supremely successful case: one in which a student has actually *become* her new persona, without reservation, no longer playing a part.

Yet Maria seemed well aware of the resemblances and

differences between Doctor Yerdeli's creation and the real life she claimed she now remembered. She kept pointing them out. And she told Doctor Yerdeli the biggest difference of all. She had a husband! Back there, in Kikiburee, a husband whom she loved was waiting for her in their old house! Above all else, she wanted to get back home again. She pleaded with Doctor Yerdeli to let her go immediately.

Doctor Yerdeli settled her down again. Could Maria remember the car accident? Yes, she said. For the first time, she had a clear memory of crossing a street in the city, a violent blow, then emptiness. Now, everything from the past had a name again, she could remember all the faces and names, even the smells, all the details of a fully lived life. And her husband! her husband! She was overwhelmed with excitement.

After hours of questioning, Doctor Yerdeli conceded. She felt a little sad at the useless expenditure of effort on what she had hoped might turn into one of her true masterpieces. But she had no doubt she would be able to adapt it for some future student. At the Institute for the Lost, no exercise of the imagination was ever wasted.

She decided to accompany Maria back to her home, to gently reintroduce her to her background. She would not warn anyone in Kikiburee in advance; it would be invaluable for research purposes to note the spontaneous reactions to Maria's return by all those who had known her previously. She had been three years at the Institute for the Lost by then.

5

They flew together to the city, rented a car, and drove two hundred miles west into the bush, to Kikiburee.

As they drew nearer the little town, Maria couldn't stop talking. She pointed out hills and creeks and peculiar clusters of gum trees, she forecast land formations and bends in the road, as only a native could. When they came to the little bush town with its board sidewalks and its wide verandas along the main street, she recognized some of the people they passed. And look! there was the little wooden gothic church of St Martin's! And behind it, the school she had taught in! And just there, further along, the grocery store she used to visit every day!

Doctor Yerdeli parked the car and they got out.

Maria rushed over to two women coming out of the store. She held out her arms.

'Judy! Heather! It's me!'

The two women did not respond to her familiarity. Being country people, they smiled politely, but in the way they would to a stranger. Doctor Yerdeli encouraged them. Didn't they remember Maria, who had lived in Kikiburee till five years ago? Perhaps she had changed a little.

They said, puzzled, no, they didn't remember her. How could they, they had never seen her before.

Maria insisted. Of course they had. Didn't she know their first names, the streets they lived on, didn't they remember growing up with her, how they had played games together, how she had often visited their homes?

One of the women was looking a little frightened by now, and the other was becoming angry that this person, who, she said, was an absolute stranger, should know so much about them.

Maria wanted to argue, but Doctor Yerdeli gently coaxed her away. She said they should go now to where Maria remembered her house had been. They walked along a shady sidestreet. And there it stood, exactly as she had described it, a small wooden house with a veranda round all four walls, a flaking turret, and gum trees overhanging.

Doctor Yerdeli knocked at the screen door. A middle-aged man with a wisp of hair and a pleasant smile pushed the door ajar and asked if he could help. He didn't give Maria a second glance.

'John!' she said.

The man looked at her.

Just then, from inside the house, a pale, dark-haired woman in an apron came to stand shyly beside him at the door, wondering who the visitors were.

'John! It's me!' Maria said again. 'I'm Maria!'

'Do I know you?' he asked.

Doctor Yerdeli saw how perplexed the man was and explained that Maria had been in an accident some years ago. She had the notion that he was her husband and that this was her house.

Maria wouldn't be kept out of it. She said it was not a notion. John and she had been married twenty years.

She could tell them anything they wanted to know about him: didn't he have a long scar on his belly that she had touched, herself, many times? Didn't he have a web-toe on his right foot, like his father before him? And what about the house? She knew the location of all the rooms, everything that was in them, the smell of the attic. Even the pictures on the walls: who did they think had bought them? Need she go on? What was wrong with everybody?

Doctor Yerdeli could see the couple was astonished at all of this. But the woman, timid as she was, spoke up. She asked how Maria could possibly be John's wife, for she herself had married him twenty-five years ago, when she was only eighteen.

Maria was the bewildered one now. The man obviously did not know her, and this woman did not seem the kind to tell a lie.

Now a dog appeared, a black and white collie, running to them from somewhere, wagging its tail at the visitors.

Maria became excited again.

'Robbie!' she said. 'Come here, Robbie!'

The dog stopped in its tracks, cowering away from her outstretched hand. It growled fiercely, baring its fangs, coat standing on end, paws trembling. The man soothed the animal. He said Robbie was indeed the dog's name, and he had always been a friendly dog. They had never seen him act like this.

Maria began to cry now, helplessly. Doctor Yerdeli took her by the arm and walked her away from the house along the shady street to the car. They drove out of Kikiburee without looking back.

6

Maria was still staring into the fetid water of the pool at the Institute for the Lost. Doctor Yerdeli patted her shoulder again.

'It's a very interesting case, and we're working on it together now,' she said to me. She looked down, brightly, at her student: 'Aren't we, Maria?'

Maria, looking more faded than ever in the bright sun, her long face straining, as though she was trying to remember something, at last glanced up at her and smiled back, half-heartedly.

As we walked away, Doctor Yerdeli talked about the case. Years of research at the Institute had convinced her that many individuals wake up each morning of their adult lives having forgotten who they are. Most of them put on a brave face and carry on, playing whatever role seems to be expected of them: husband, waitress, bank manager, teacher, bus driver. They become skilled at gauging their situation. Without panic, they adapt themselves. This was a daily, common occurrence.

'A man like you must have . . . experienced it,' she said.

I could not tell whether this was a question or a statement.

Doctor Yerdeli wondered if what had happened to Maria in Kikiburee might not be a variation of the problem. Might not an entire community suffer this kind of memory lapse? Was it not conceivable that Maria had indeed once lived in Kikiburee, but that all of the townspeople there had adjusted their memories to exclude her, the way we exclude certain unpleasant smells? Indeed, Doctor Yerdeli speculated, people like Maria might have a certain lack, a metaphysical deficiency, possibly, that induced this type of amnesia on the part of others. Perhaps instances of the phenomenon were widespread yet went completely unnoticed, because of our tendency to trust the collective memory rather than the individual's. Was it not possible that not only communities, but even countries, even whole civilizations might be subject to the phenomenon?

As she presented these possibilities, she was gesticulating as usual, so that I could not help noticing those little blue numbers tatooed above her wrist. She said she would be addressing an international congress on her theory soon, and was in the process of setting up some models for testing.

I considered asking her this question: 'Wouldn't it be better, in the case of someone like Maria, just to let her go out into the world on her own and start a new life from scratch, without stocking her mind with inventions?'

But I didn't ask. I was certain she would have some confident, expert reply, such as: 'No, that would be very unwise. Nothing is more dangerous to civilization than those who lack memories.'

And then what could I have said?

7

Looking at me shrewdly, she asked if I would like to meet her most fascinating student, one of her 'Director's Pets.' I said I would be only too happy.

We crossed to the building on the ocean side, and climbed the breezy stairway to the second floor. She took me to one of the rooms that looked eastward, out onto the tops of palm trees. We could hear, vaguely, the sound of breakers beyond the lagoon. She knocked and opened the door.

'Good day, Harry,' she said in a cheerful voice. And we went in.

He was sitting upright in his pyjamas in a chair: a thin, bearded man, with dark hair and dark-rimmed, frightened eyes that were constantly scanning the room. There was a smell, perhaps of stale sweat, that even the open window did not dispel. The man paid no direct attention to us, but occasionally moved his head slightly to look past us and round us, as though, at times, we were blocking his view.

This was Harry, she said, formerly a successful lawyer, with a wife and two children. Some time ago, in bed one night, he heard noises coming from somewhere in his house. He got up to see what was going on, thinking it must be the children. But they were both fast asleep. His wife told him she couldn't hear any noise at all. He asked her to listen. Was she sure, if she listened very carefully, she couldn't hear a sound? Like someone shouting, but muffled, so that the words were incomprehensible? She told him no, he must be imagining things. So he lay there for hours, straining his ears, till he fell asleep out of sheer exhaustion.

This went on for weeks. Harry was losing a lot of sleep, nothing more serious than that. During the day, everything was normal.

Then, one morning, when he was at his desk in the city, wearily going over some documents, he heard the distant shouting again. That was the first time he had ever heard it outside his own home, or in the light of day. He checked with his secretary. No, she could hear nothing. What about his partner, his old friend? No, nothing at all. They told him not to worry, perhaps he was under stress.

And he didn't worry too much. Until he began seeing something. Just a glimpse, but something, both in his own house and at the office. If he looked up suddenly, he'd catch a glimpse of it, just for a second, almost like an after-vision left by a light switched off. He thought it was a man. In fact, he was sure it was a man, but it was hard to say, he couldn't catch sight of it for long enough.

Though it was often nearby, sitting on the spare chair at the dinner-table, or in the passenger seat of the car, or standing by his desk. Disappearing before Harry could get a clear view of it.

He, by now, had learnt from his past experience. He told his wife and his children, just once, what he had seen. And asked them, just once, if they had spotted a stranger prowling around the house, outside. Or inside.

As he feared, they had not. He didn't mention the subject again. In fact, when his wife asked him, later, if he was still seeing things, he laughed. Clogged sinuses, he said, the problem must be his clogged sinuses.

But as the weeks went by, she noticed, they all noticed, that often, as Harry was doing some routine thing, eating his meals, or reading legal documents, or speaking on the telephone, or even in the middle of small-talk with one of them, he would suddenly become alert, straining his ears. Or he would turn his head sharply and look past them, his eyes wide with alarm. Yet, if they asked him what was wrong, he would say everything was just fine.

Within another month, he was completely useless. He spent all his time, day and night, listening to the distant shouting, trying to get a good look at something no one else could see. More and more, now, his eyes were filled with fear.

He recovered immediately they took him away to the coast for a week's holiday. He was his old self again, making love to his wife for the first time in months, playing with the children the way he used to in the old days. Till one afternoon while he was at the beach helping

75

them build a sandcastle, whatever it was caught up with him. He sat for the rest of the week, in the hotel, without saying a word, engrossed in his private torment.

They took him home again on a Monday. That day, he spoke for the last time, just as darkness was falling, the time he feared most. He spoke to his wife with the studied effort of a man tearing himself away from some dreadful preoccupation. But he spoke clearly, and struggled to repeat himself, to make sure she understood. No one, he said, should worry about him. He would fight to the end, he would protect them, he would not let them down.

She wept and asked him what he meant. But he could not speak again.

From that day, almost a year before, all his attention was focused on that other voice, that invisible companion he seemed so fearful of.

Six months ago, desperate, all other treatments having failed, his wife brought him to the Institute for the Lost. At their first meeting, Doctor Yerdeli, on an impulse, put her stethoscope to the top of Harry's head. From inside, she heard quite plainly a sound. Like a distant voice roaring. She decided immediately to take him on as one of her 'Specials.'

Doctor Yerdeli, at that point, offered me her stethoscope, so that I myself might listen. She said Harry would not mind at all.

I declined.

The case fascinated her. She and one of her assistants were making tapes of the sound in Harry's head, amplified through the stethoscope. A computer was in the process of analysing them. She hoped for the results any day now.

Had I noticed, she asked, how Harry's eyes roved constantly as though he was tracking the movements of something else in the room, some third guest that we couldn't see? And how terrified he seemed to be? Well, some weeks ago, she had called in a specialist to construct an optometric device to measure the refractions in Harry's eyes. The data gathered so far had been fed into a computer. They hoped to be able to make a composite figure, on the screen, of what Harry was looking at. After a few more sessions, the specialist expected he would have a very good idea of what it was. So far, even from the incomplete data, all he could say was that the body on the screen seemed human, but not necessarily the head.

8

As we left that room, with its inbred smell and the man, Harry, sitting there, absorbed in his fearsome, private world, I must admit to a certain sense of relief. Walking along the corridor, I asked Doctor Yerdeli:

'Why did you take him in?'

'You can't be careful enough in matters such as this,' she replied, looking at me in her shrewd way.

I thought about that.

'And if you were to discover what the voice is saying, and what the thing looks like, what then?' For I could sense that she felt that no one in all the world was better equipped than she was to deal with Harry's problem.

'You, of course, think it would be . . . better just to leave it alone, trapped inside him?' she said.

And when I said yes, I did think so, she only shook her head, and shook it again and again. She smiled at me, a cheerful smile.

'Ah, it's so rarely I meet . . . optimists,' she said.

And would discuss the case no further.

9

The day had not been a dull one for me, so I accepted her invitation to have dinner at her bungalow, instead of flying back to the mainland at five o'clock as I had intended.

After a good meal, we sat on wicker chairs on the veranda, smelling the sea and the coffee, watching the reef aerate the incoming waves. The palm trees were curtsying to a pleasant easterly that kept the mosquitoes down. The sudden tropical night fell as Doctor Yerdeli was telling me about her youth in Europe, her training, her condemnation and imprisonment, her escape. And her return.

'I went back there, years after the war was over. It was very foolish of me. I was hoping for the impossible. I found . . . nothing. There was nothing left.'

She lingered over the nothings.

'I hoped most of all that my dog, Rex, would be waiting for me. Isn't that strange? But of course, even if they did not kill him, he would have died of old age, long before.'

She sipped her coffee.

'For a long time after that, I used to ask myself, does it really matter? Either way, there is no . . . constancy. I had to learn again to believe in constancy.'

Women in her profession were rare, and she had trouble getting a job. She found one in this part of the world, in a little jungle hospital, where she spent her time trying to understand the forms of madness peculiar to those who live their lives in jungles.

In the dim light of the veranda, I sensed suddenly that she was looking at me very intently. The way I had seen her look at her students. And for the first time, I wondered if she had any ulterior motive for asking me to stay for dinner.

She said she thought I might want to hear about a case she had encountered in those early days. A man who was not a native. He was a very elderly European who had undergone a trauma up in the highlands, amongst the head-hunters.

'He would have been a . . . marvellous student for the Institute, if it had existed then. If we could have saved him.'

She was watching me. She enunciated her words emphatically.

'His name was Amos Mackenzie.'

The name alerted me immediately. Mainly because it was not long since I had told the Patagonian story to Helen. And because, only a few weeks ago, I had asked Donald Cromarty to investigate the story. On the other hand, I knew the world was full of Mackenzies.

But I was curious, so I asked, 'Amos Mackenzie?'

'Yes, that's right. He was an old man. He came, I remember, from your part of the world. Have you heard of him?'

Suddenly, I felt the need to be careful.

'There are so many Mackenzies from my part of the world. Did you talk to him?'

The veranda light was not strong, but I could see she was still watching for my reaction. Whatever she saw, she decided not to ask me any more questions.

'He did the talking, mainly. About his experience up in the high jungle. It must have been a . . . difficult journey for a man of his age.'

She sipped at her coffee, studying again her mental notepad, finding the words to fit. And I myself relaxed, thinking that it was very improbable, to say the least, the old man could have been one of those Patagonian Mackenzies. I just sipped my own coffee, and listened.

She said that when Amos Mackenzie was brought to the hospital, the resident, after doing what he could, was very relieved to be able to ask for her, to see if she could help. Mackenzie had been carried in by some hunters who'd come across him in the jungle, in a terrible condition.

She remembered how he looked, lying there in a bed in the little tin-roofed hospital. He was a tall man (she could assess a man's height, even lying down), emaciated, his skin like bark, at least seventy years old, though it was hard to tell, for he was one of those who look as though they've always been old.

She had no trouble getting him to talk and that was good. He was an articulate man with a reedy voice and seemed happy to have an audience. He said he'd been on an archaeological expedition to one of those remote areas between the maps (he used that phrase), on the banks of the Merape . . .

10

. . . on the banks of the Merape, I sweated, along with my colleagues, to uncover several small pyramids, just fifty feet high, overgrown for centuries by jungle. Dangerous brown snakes lived in their geometrical corridors. In that region, we kept finding great egg-shaped rocks hewn out of some kind of limestone. They were as high as lanu trees, but they were hard to see from any distance because of the thick jungle.

We thought at first they were just peculiar earthmounds till we noticed how the bottoms were indented behind the loose curtain of vines. The brown snakes lived there too.

These things we had all seen the likes of before, but in other parts of the world. Never here, in this country. We had no theories to account for them.

The weather was awful. In the late afternoons, just when the heat was at its worst and the humidity most oppressive, the rain would start and would pour down hour after hour till dark. The trees gave us no protection, for their leaves, high above, just stored the drops long enough to allow them to accumulate greater weight. We would keep on digging, nevertheless, though we were attacked by the innumerable mosquitoes and stinging flies the rain seemed to encourage.

On our last day at that site, about dusk, we found a stone hand. We had seen the overgrown mound, and thought it was probably the same as the others, though more mis-shapen. But as we hacked at the vegetation with machetes, careful to avoid snakes, we saw the huge stubby fingers protruding through their glove of vines. They seemed to be clutching at the air, the gesture of a giant drowning in quicksand. We were all astonished to find such an object here, so far from any known civilization.

But it was not just a hand. With twenty-foot long prods, we thrust down into the soil around it, and could feel, down there, the outlines of an arm, a shoulder, a head. We speculated that the entire figure must be seventy feet tall, and must have been interred upright in this pit, only the hand left above ground. We felt apprehensive. But we were all too rational, too engrossed in our work.

The morning after, the sky was still overcast, the jungle silent as ever. We launched the boats on the brown river and pushed on further upstream.

They attacked us about six miles upstream, where the Merape waters were dark brown and narrow, and where the jungle rose high on either side, like unending book-cases full of the same books. We were near to the east bank and had no sign of their presence. Then, the air was full of spears, and arrows, and howls from the bank. We tried to paddle away, but dark arms burst out of the water under our boats and seized the gunwales. Some of them had been hiding in the water, breathing through reeds, waiting.

Then, I was in the water too, lashing out at the mad faces and the hands that were grasping, pulling me under. I breathed deep and dived. I could see nothing, except perhaps the outline of one of those evil figures clutching at me. I kicked at it, and kept swimming.

Fear made me endure. When I surfaced, I was fifty yards downstream. I could see, back there, the water thrashing as though fish were being gathered in a net, and I could hear screams. I plunged under again, and when I came up, I did not look back, but kept swimming with the current, choosing the river dangers rather than the treacherous shore.

How long I stayed in the river, or how far I went, I do not know. But in time, I could hear again the monotonous shrieking of jungle birds, a sound I had not heard for so long, and knew I had better begin to work my way towards the bank, the west bank. It was by then completely shaded, so sunset must have been near. I swam towards some mud-flats where I thought I might be able to rest for the night. I thought no further ahead than sleep. I was fearless from exhaustion. I crawled out of the Merape onto the wet bank and, in spite of the stench of the mud, fell asleep immediately.

When I woke, a chaos of devil faces hovered over me, and I knew with certainty that before long I would die painfully. The Ishtulum had found me. I recognized them by their tribal paint and war-hats as the most savage of all the tribes along the Merape. A group of them stood round me, prodding with their spear-hurlers at my white skin, a diseased whiteness to their dark eyes. They bound my hands, and dragged me back to their village. Before them lay a long ritual cleansing of the pollution of their territory and the ritual elimination of the polluter, me. Like many a traveller who falls into the hands of the Ishtulum, I wished that they had killed me with their spears.

For the next three weeks, I was kept closely guarded in the centre of their village, tethered at the ankles to a lanu tree. Yet I cannot say I was lonely. For a tribe so ferocious, the Ishtulum are garrulous, they love to talk, and made no effort to hide their secrets from a stranger sentenced to death.

Their shaman, for example, has an eye in the back of his head. I saw this eye many times, whenever the shaman, in his cloak of feathers and painted face, would turn his back on me and would strain this painful and bloodshot organ to look me over. One of my guards told me that the wives of the shaman select a child of four or five years old to be his successor. Over a period of about ten years, they gradually coax the child's left eye from its socket, millimetre by millimetre, stretching the eye ligaments till the ball of the eye nestles behind the left ear. It lies there, wrapped in a constantly oiled banana skin which is attached to his head by a cord.

Though the sight in the shaman's rear eye is not acute, it is powerful in other ways and is the eye members of the tribe fear most. They say it looks into the house of the dead. They say it can paralyse the enemies of the Ishtulum. Its wavering, disembodied gaze centred on me all too often.

I learnt too that for the Ishtulum, certain animals are extensions of human beings, almost extra limbs. Like many of the better-known tribes in that region of the Merape, they keep tiny monkeys in their hair to devour fleas and lice. But they go further. At puberty, each boy must swallow a small blue lizard about eight inches long, which will live inside his stomach for the period of one moon. The boy has to lie as still as possible for fear of causing the death of the lizard. He may drink only water, and may defecate only with great care. The Ishtulum believe that if the lizard dies while in his stomach, the boy's own spirit will die within minutes. My guards told me they had all seen such deaths.

From my lanu tree, I had a good view of the ceremony at which these lizards are withdrawn. I had been a captive for just a few days at the time. One day, when the sun was at its height, eight boys were carried on stretchers from their huts by family members and placed in a circle. The shaman appeared, still dressed in his coat of feathers, but with his face painted vividly for the occasion to look like a reptile. His rear eye was tucked away, the ligaments trailing along the side of his head and disappearing into the empty eye-cavern. He danced and chanted for a while, then began the ceremonial withdrawal of the lizards. He took a long, thin piece of twine and tied on a little yellow fruit fly, the lizard's favourite food. Humming a noisy prayer, he fed the twine down the throat of the first boy, who lay still and tense.

The shaman paused, then began gently to pull on the twine, like a fisherman, while the boy started to repeat over and over his family name. The tribe watched in absolute silence. In a moment, we could see the head of the lizard at the boy's mouth. The shaman plucked it out quickly and gave it to one of his assistants who carefully placed it in a wicker basket.

I was filled with admiration for the shaman's skill. Any clumsiness by him might result in the lizard's refusal of the fly, meaning death for the boy. This day, all was going well. The lizards were successfully and quickly coaxed out of seven boys undergoing the rite. The boys lay there, weak, relieved that the ordeal was over, and the members of the tribe began to relax.

But the shaman was having trouble with the eighth boy. His lizard was not responding in spite of numerous jiggings of the twine. The boy kept repeating his family name, trying not to sob. The shaman eventually attached a fresh fly to the twine. Still no response. I could see on the faces of the Ishtulum their fear that the lizard inside the boy was dead.

But the shaman would not admit defeat. He stood up and, with a dramatic gesture, uncovered his rear eye. He glared through it at the boy for many minutes. Then he tucked the eye back in the banana skin, and bent over the trembling body. He inserted the twine again, waited for a while, and began to tug gently. The boy continued repeating his family name over and over like an incantation, till very gradually, the sound changed to a gurgle, as the shaman withdrew from the throat a lizard that looked none too healthy. Even under all that paint, we could see the jubilation on the shaman's ghastly face. If he had not succeeded on the third try, that would have been that, and the boy would have died soon after. The Ishtulum roared their joy. I think they marvelled at the shaman's skill, but even more at the boy for withstanding direct exposure to that grotesque eye. Only the imminence of death could have given him the courage.

That gastric experience at puberty prepares the Ishtulum males for another intimate relationship, entered into not long after, between a warrior and a small rodent, a type of coatimundi.

I had noticed that if my guard was an unmarried man, he would have one of these creatures attached by a small gold ring to the tip of his penis. The coatimundi would feed on the semen of its owner. Whenever the guard masturbated (the Ishtulum are prodigious masturbators, and guards would no sooner appear for duty than they would begin this exercise, quite conscientiously), his coatimundi would clean up the spill. It seems, also, though I did not witness this myself, that when an unmarried warrior makes love to one of the women, his coatimundi, clinging to his erect penis, enters the vagina of the woman first and gobbles up all the seminal fluids. I could not help admiring this very practical way of ensuring that no children are born out of wedlock, or before the proper potlatch has been arranged.

When a marriage ceremony is performed, the shaman again plays an important role. He formally snips off the rodent's ring, thus permitting fruitful union. As in the case of those lizards at puberty, it is very bad luck if a man's coatimundi dies before the official snipping. The Ishtulum take it to mean either that the semen of its owner is sour, or that it is not strong enough to keep his animal alive. The man may not marry within the tribe.

They call marriage the linking. No sooner has the man been freed from his coatimundi than he is linked to his bride in such a way that infidelity would be very difficult. The shaman is again the central figure. Before the assembled tribe, he sews together the flap of skin between the thumb and the forefinger of the man's left hand and the woman's right hand. He uses a thin needle made of fishbone and a twine made of gut. The stitching only takes a few minutes, and, since they are Ishtulum, the couple shows no sign of pain as he joins their flesh. For the first six months of their marriage they are obliged to do everything together. He is with her as she cooks, eats, gardens, urinates, defecates, menstruates.

She, in turn, goes with him through the hazards of the hunt, the weekly palm-beer-drinking orgies, and, if she is unlucky enough, the inter-tribal wars.

After six months, when the woman is advanced in pregnancy, the shaman carefully separates the couple's hands, leaving only a wedding scar. She goes off to join the other women in preparation for her child-birth.

I wondered at first why some of the older members of the tribe still had their hands linked. I found out that these were the childless couples, their hands sewn together for life. Everyone treats them with great kindness, though nothing can make up for the tragedy of their barrenness.

But there was no kindness to spare for me, at least not as I then understood the word. And I expected none. After three weeks, with the whole tribe present, the guards took me from my tether at the lanu tree and spreadeagled me on a low wooden frame to which the shaman tied me with ritual knots. His incantations became louder. The final purification process had begun.

With a sliver of razor-bamboo, he began making little incisions over much of the front of my body. When he was satisfied that he had made enough of them, he wiped the sliver carefully, gave it to his assistant, and moved on to the next process. With the fingertips of his left hand, he spread the cuts open slightly, and with his right hand forced in small quantities of dirt which mixed with the blood. Then, he began to stuff into the incisions a variety of seedlings of jungle plants and trees, chanting while he worked.

I remained conscious during this painful process. He performed all of the intricate operations with his back to me, relying upon his uncovered rear eye. When he bent over me, he smelt like a jungle animal. The assembled tribe, exerting their collective power in these purifications, also kept their backs to the ceremony. The only Ishtulum eye that watched me was that bloodshot eye in the back of the shaman's head. I am certain I saw in it compassion at my pain and despair.

For a whole week I was left lying on that frame in the middle of the village. But now the members of the tribe were permitted to look at me from a distance. Every few hours, the shaman himself would come and sprinkle a bad-smelling mixture on the plants that protruded from me, and force a few spoonfuls of it into my mouth.

At first the plants drooped feebly, and he had a worried look. But after two days, they seemed to spring to life, as all jungle plants do, and began to grow in the cuts. I think they drew nourishment from the pus in my sores. Eventually, I could sense a tickling sensation inside of me as the tiny roots groped around for places to attach themselves. I could feel my body being turned into a garden.

At the end of that week, on a fine morning, the whole tribe assembled again. Six of the strongest warriors, chanting rhythmically, lifted me on my frame. They carried me in procession to the river bank, a half-mile north of the village, to the place where they had found me. My little plants were gently weaving in the morning breeze as though the Ishtulum were moving a rack at a plant nursery.

Beside the river, on the dry mud just above high water, a shallow grave had already been dug into which they lowered me, still on my frame. The shaman, chanting to the river, covered my body softly with the fertile soil, leaving only my little plants and my face exposed.

I understood. I was to grow into the soil in the very place I had contaminated, returning myself to nature all cleansed and blessed, amending the pollution I had caused.

Before they left, each member of the tribe, mumbling prayers, came and looked down at me with, I thought, forgiveness, and even affection. Then they were gone and I was alone.

I lay there for three entire days and nights, watching and feeling my plants grow tall and strong. I was contented that they were so healthy I could feel their longing to rejoin the jungle soil beneath my body. Sometimes I would try to speak to them, encourage them, but my words became a trembling of branches, a sighing of leaves. Insects were beginning to build their nests in my plants, and once a small bird with a worm in its mouth landed on my favourite tree, the dwarf suma growing from the middle of my chest. The bird stared down into my eyes for a while, quite unafraid.

On the third day, I could feel my entire body begin to take root in the river soil under and around me. I could even feel the fingers of my own hand growing down, down. It was what I had been waiting for, or, should I say, what *we* had been waiting for. I knew then that nothing remained but to think no more, just allow myself to grow into that fertile earth, accept what was no longer pain but an intensity of pleasure no living human being had ever before enjoyed. My whole body had become part of a universal, endless orgasm.

Then I woke here, in this hospital. Some hunters, it seems, had found me staked out, still alive. They had hacked away the foliage from me (my poor children!), and brought me here. The surgeons gather round me in a ring for tortuous hours each day, cutting the roots out of me, leaving my body burning. When I am alone at last, I lie here looking out of the window and watch, only a few hundred yards away, my jungle, my love, waiting for me patiently, no matter what they do, welcoming me in the end.

11

'There was not a mark on him,' said Doctor Yerdeli. 'But whatever his disease was, it was too . . . virulent to be cured by any words I know. I could do nothing. He lived a few days longer, and then he died, cradling his stomach. We buried him at the edge of the jungle.'

'Did he have any scars at all? Was there a scar of any kind on his abdomen?'

She looked at me with those shrewd eyes.

'I never saw one. Why do you ask?'

I gave no reason, and I asked no more questions. She was the kind of woman I didn't wish to confide in. Though I was certain, by now, that she had no other ulterior motive for inviting me for dinner than to talk to me and look me over. I think she regarded everybody as a potential student, and something about me must have made her hopeful.

I sat silently, allowing myself to wonder if this Amos Mackenzie really was a member of the Patagonian Mackenzies. Wouldn't that be remarkable? The past, in an odd way, seems to depend so much upon the future: everything would be different, somehow, if it were to turn out that those Mackenzies my grandfather had told me about really did exist.

Doctor Yerdeli was still watching me closely, so I tried to close my face to her as though it was a hand and she was a reader of palms. I was sure she had the art to decipher a whole life history in a face.

I made a fuss about looking at my watch and being surprised at how late it was. I said good-night and goodbye, and retreated to the safety of the guest-house.

I never saw her again. I flew out of the island early the next morning. As the plane circled before heading south-west to the city, the ocean beneath was misty and flat, and the island was like a blot on a huge grey page on which nothing had yet been written, or everything had been erased.

12

Answers depend upon questioners. A passenger on the plane home asked me about my trip, and I chatted about blue skies and seas, beaches and reefs, palm trees and trade winds.

To tell Helen such things would be to tell her nothing at all. On the night I arrived home, we made love with great tenderness: I was so happy to be home again, and to be loved. Then I told her about Doctor Yerdeli and the Institute for the Lost, about the neglected swimming pool, about Maria and Kikiburee, about Harry's invisible torment. And finally, I told her about Amos Mackenzie and the Ishtulum.

She was as surprised at that part of it as I had been.

Her head lay on my chest, and I was stroking her fair hair, breathing in her scent, soothing her smooth shoulder and back. We could see night clouds through the big window, imagining them to be various creatures and shapes, not content to let them be what they were.

I said, thinking of Amos Mackenzie:

'If he really was one of those Mackenzies, you could almost believe there was some pattern behind it all.'

'Perhaps,' she said.

'When Doctor Yerdeli started talking about him, I felt strange, as though I had stepped back into something important in my own past.'

She kissed me gently, as I continued in this philosophic mood.

'Perhaps I was remembering how my life was when I was a boy. What it was like to hope. Maybe it was the memory of once being full of hopes that made me feel so strange.'

Helen was silent for a long time. I thought perhaps I had made her sad. But when she spoke, it was about Amos Mackenzie. She said it was futile of him to have believed his life could be transformed into trees and plants. When all that was left of him was a story, in words. When words are, in a way, our only lasting blossoms.

I liked the idea that words were blossoms. How sometimes, somebody gathers the most pleasing of them and preserves them. I told Helen so. This was the kind of conversation we used to have, and used to enjoy so much. And, as always, at a certain point, she began laughing, and snuggled in, and before we knew it we were again involved in a form of grafting peculiar to men and women.

Afterwards, I promised myself (I still had not told Helen) I'd write to Donald Cromarty once more and let him know that I'd heard about the life and death of one Amos Mackenzie, who might have been a member of the Patagonian Mackenzies. Perhaps the information would be of some value to him in his research into my grandfather's story. I did not then realize how he would use all these things, at the Paradise Motel. I turned on my side, inhaling the sweet scent of Helen, and went to sleep, and slept that night as well as I have ever slept.

Part Three

RACHEL

Rachel Mackenzie and her older sister, Esther, spent several years in the Border country, at St Fiona's Home for Waifs and Strays (for girls only), run by the Sisters of the Holy Order of Correction. From the start, Rachel was a very withdrawn child, which was a good thing in an institution where catatonia passed easily for obedience and docility. When she was fourteen, she was already beautiful, slim, and delicate.

She took to sitting for hours each day in the darkened boiler-room of the orphanage. She told Esther, her sister, that she did this because she could feel herself splitting into pieces, evaporating in the daylight. The darkness left her intact.

As she grew more beautiful, she spoke less frequently and used simpler words. But her sister and the other orphans found it was ever harder to understand what she meant. Her beauty was so jarring in that arid place that everyone was relieved when it was time for her to depart.

She went to the capital, where she found a series of jobs till she had earned enough to enrol in night classes to learn typing. She had many lovers in this period. They were permitted to enter her body, but never her mind.

She met the rest of her family only once

after leaving the orphanage. She sailed for North America in the year of her twenty-fifth birthday, on the *Mauritius*. She stayed in her cabin with her portholes covered on all but the dullest days. On land again, she travelled by train into the interior of the continent in a private compartment with the blinds drawn. On arrival at her destination, at night, she was relieved to find the quality of the darkness had not diminished, but if anything, improved with the distance travelled.

Notebook, A. McGAW

1

Two, or perhaps three months later, on a day when Helen had gone up to the city, I drove down to the country house of JP. He was a very old man (at least eighty), very elegant, with slick silver hair. In fact, it would not be going too far to say he exuded a kind of silveriness: silver skin, silver voice, a slight silver smile. I wanted to talk to him about a woman photographer, long dead herself, who had specialized in taking pictures of those who were dying. She had occasionally worked for JP when he owned a large newspaper in the city. But he remembered nothing about her. Anyway, he was an old man who was more interested in talking about his own experiences.

We sat at either end of a couch in a room that smelt faintly of aftershave, and was furnished with comfortable modern furniture and machinery: in one corner, a stereo and a shelf of records; on a table beside us, a crouching ivory-coloured telephone. It never rang while I was there. From time to time as he talked, I could see horse-drawn buggies, all black, easing their way along the road at the end of his driveway. They were of a kind used by a religious sect that still farmed this area. Watching them from this side of JP's window was like watching a movie with a period setting. I said, for the sake of conversation, that it must feel strange to live in close proximity to such an anachronism. He breathed for a moment. The idea, he said, did not excite him any more or less than did the notion that the solid continents we inhabit are slowly drifting, or that we are spinning helplessly, all our lives around the sun.

I gave up my efforts at small talk. He had more to say, however, on the subject. He said he was, perhaps, a man nothing could surprise any more. He had heard others suggest that in old age, everything ought to be a surprise, even waking up in the morning; perhaps as a defence against such a barrage of surprises, some men develop surprise-proof exteriors that are easily mistaken for complacence. Even by the individuals themselves.

2

'Then again,' he said, 'perhaps I lost my innocence too early.'

When he was a boy, he said, in another country, living on his father's farm, it was customary to go out in the autumn, hunting rabbits. Some of the men would use a combination of guns and demonic little ferrets. They would set their trained ferrets loose in the warrens to panic the rabbits out onto the guns.

But JP's father would allow neither guns nor ferrets on his property. He preferred to trap the rabbits. His method was to set snares, tiny gallows with wooden uprights and wire nooses, in the well-trodden rabbit paths. The snares would be left overnight, and next day he and JP would collect the catch.

JP, as a boy, half-enjoyed the trapping, though he was half-sorry for the rabbits. He thought it a gesture of kindness in his father to use snares: at least the rabbits had some hope of avoiding them. He told his father so. He laughed and patted JP on the head (he was then about twelve). JP's mother was the one who insisted on the snares, he said, and not out of any sense of fair play to the rabbits. On the contrary, she believed there was no treat like a rabbit caught overnight in a snare; the flesh turned so tender it was a delight. She said it had something to do with the duration of the rabbit's suffering. Guns killed them too quickly.

JP's tongue was a small silver blade flicking along his lips, slitting his face open from the inside to let the words slide out.

'If duration of suffering had the same effect on human beings, what tasty morsels we would make,' he said. I was not certain whether he was referring to the two of us, sitting side by side on his pleasant couch in that modern room, or to the world in general. I felt a little uncomfortable at the knowing look he gave me with those silvery eyes.

Suffering was one thing, he said. But what about death? He had seen his fill of deaths. Bloody deaths, as much as any man. Especially during the period when he was a war correspondent. That was long ago. But there were other deaths, the more remarkable in peacetime. He had retained what might be considered sentimental recollections of two of them, both violent: one of a man, the other of a woman.

The first happened when he was a cub reporter down here in one of the big country-towns. It was a clear case of suicide. Yet, a man would have hanged for it if he had not stopped to buy a cigar.

'Let me show you something,' JP said, getting to his feet a little stiffly (the silver had entered his joints). He went to a cabinet beside his writing table. He riffled through a drawer, then came back to the sofa, holding a sheet of paper that was yellow with age. A brief message was typed on it in an old fashioned type-face:

> I am afraid for my life.
> Jack Miller has threatened to kill me
> if I don't pay him back his money.
> Don't let him get away with it.
> For God's sake.

The note was signed, in pen and ink, in a small, neat hand – 'General Lundt.' Lundt, said JP, was the one who killed himself. Jack Miller was the man who might have hanged.

The note had been acquired by JP when the inquest into Lundt's death was over and the case closed. The police let him keep it, for a half-dozen similar notes had turned up.

Lundt had sent them all over the place, to his doctor, his lawyer, his co-workers, to arrive in the mail on the day after his death.

'Each note said the same thing: that Lundt was afraid Miller would kill him.' JP leaned back, his silvery eyes half-shut. 'In those days, if Miller had done it, he'd have been hanged by a villager from Basden just five miles south of here.'

I knew he would tell me now about Basden, though I would have preferred to hear about Lundt. I wondered if, in his mind, things were connected, if there were no digressions. Or perhaps directness was too unsophisticated, too blunt for a man like him. Or perhaps the path through his memory was criss-crossed by so many half-forgotten intersections and dead ends he could no longer walk with complete certainty to his destination. At any rate, he was leaning back on the couch, flexing the long silvery fingers of his right hand so that they rustled, the way dry bone would rustle inside loose skin.

3

Basden, he said, was a small village of fieldstone houses, nearby. All the public executioners in the last hundred years had been members of one family, the Morrisons, and had lived in the village for several generations. JP himself once interviewed two of the Morrison brothers during the peak years of the hanging era. He had been apprehensive about meeting them, but the brothers, slimly built with flaming red hair, were quite normal and cheerful. The village took great pride in them, and had named the children's playground with its swings and maypole after them.

The brothers were certainly conscientious about their work. They practised for three hours a day on a fully equipped gallows in their basement (they took JP down to see it, and allowed him to try out the lever; the crash of the trapdoor echoed in his ears for days after), and kept themselves in shape by jogging and weight-lifting. They showed JP an illuminated family Bible with a list, inside the cover, of four generations of family members who had been executioners on two continents.

These Morrison brothers wanted JP to know they were 'platform men': whenever they were hired, their sole responsibility was to make sure the gallows were mechanically flawless, and to perform the hanging expertly. They would never consent to clearing up underneath the platform afterwards. Victims of hangings tended to lose control of their bowels as they dropped. To say nothing of the fact that in the case of a hanged woman, the uterus would almost invariably keep on falling after the body itself had jerked to a stop at the bottom of the rope. Certain work, the Morrisons felt, was better left to house-cleaners.

Years after the first interview, and not long after capital punishment had since been abolished, JP met these same Morrison men again. They were as cheerful as ever, operating their own market-garden stall in the town, specializing in tomatoes. JP asked them what they thought of the abolition. The younger brother (they were both old by then) said he really did not mind, he still had his wonderful memories. But the elder mourned the passing of their profession. It wasn't as if killing had stopped since abolition, he said. The only difference was that nowadays almost every killing was performed by a bungler. He himself, he said, would rather be hanged by an expert than mutilated by an amateur with a sawn-off shotgun, up some back alley.

JP was smiling at the memory. 'I have a copy of my interview in my files,' he said, 'if you'd like to read it.' At times, his skin reminded me of a snake's when it is near shedding. I wondered if he had a true colour, or just another layer of silver underneath.

4

'Of course, in the Lundt case,' he said, 'there was no hanging. But there might have been.'

Lundt, he remembered as being middle-aged, bald, not handsome (JP had actually known him by sight), a clerk in the Roads Department at City Hall, an avid reader of detective novels, an unmarried man who avoided people as much as possible. Jack Miller, Lundt's supervisor, on the other hand, was not at all shy. He had ambitions to rise in the public service, he was a ladies' man, a hunter, a gambler. He had little to do with his staff, especially the male staff, and least of all with the most retiring of them, Lundt.

The night Lundt stole a pistol, a black Beretta, from Miller's collection of guns (it was the first criminal act of his life) was the night of the annual Christmas party for the Roads Department, held in Miller's own house. While all the other guests were being sociable, Lundt went prowling. In the basement, in a dark corner, he came across a glass-doored cabinet containing Miller's guns. The Beretta glistened lethally at him.

The sight of that pistol transformed Lundt. Lying there on its shelf, clean and conclusive, it told him everything. He wrapped the pistol and some bullets in his chequered handkerchief and slipped them into his pocket. He was a thief. He was prepared to be worse.

'Lundt,' said JP, 'had merely joined the human race. My father, when I was young, often said to me: look around you my boy; look at the world, with its thousands upon thousands of years of wars, plagues, famines, murders, public and private brutalities, injustices, parricides, genocides: one would have to be a cynic not to believe there was some great plan behind it all.'

JP smiled. I thought of a crocodile with its jaw slightly parted. He blinked once or twice.

5

For two weeks following the theft of the Beretta, JP said, Lundt was happier than he had ever been. His work at the office and his obsessive reading of detective stories had always seemed so unrelated: parallel roads leading to different towns. Now, miraculously, the roads met. He knew that this was the moment he had been training for all his life. During his lunch breaks at the office, when no one was around to disturb him, he prepared the trap. First, he typed letters to himself, mimicking the crude style and bad spelling of Miller, then forged his supervisor's large, easily imitable hand. The letters contained threatening statements by Miller, demanding repayment of a gambling debt.

Lundt was careful to spread the dates of the supposed correspondence over a few months. The eventual killing must not seem an impulsive act. He placed these letters around various drawers of his desk, so that they would be found in an investigation. He knew there would be an investigation. Then he typed his 'replies,' in which he begged Miller for time to pay off his debts. He tore up the originals of the 'replies,' but kept carbon copies prominently in his filing cabinet.

His next step was to confide, or pretend to confide, in some people at the office. He let it be known that for years he had been gambling heavily, the passion of a lonely man, and was now in some kind of trouble. Later that week, he visited his doctor and asked for sleeping pills to help him through a bout of depression. He allowed his doctor to prise out of him the fact that his depression was caused by gambling debts. Lundt then paid a call on his lawyer to ask what would be the best thing for a man to do, if he was threatened. The lawyer suspected that Lundt himself was the man in question.

To conclude this stage of his plan, Lundt went to the police station and made inquiries about the kind of protection they could offer a man afraid for his life. He was so jittery the policeman who spoke to him had no doubt he was talking about himself.

On the day he had chosen for the killing, a slushy January day, Lundt did not go to work. Around noon, he phoned Miller himself. This was the key moment. In his most timid voice, he asked Miller to come to the City Hall, to Lundt's own office, at exactly eight o'clock that night. He said, whispering into the phone, that he had found information on a land scandal that

110

would ruin Miller's only opponent in the next council election.

Lundt understood his man well. Jack Miller could not resist the bait. He said he'd be there at eight. He did not even wonder why Lundt would want to do him a favour. He was the kind of man who expected favours, who was too cocky even to suspect that he was hated.

'Miller,' JP said, 'was a man with little imagination. Lundt was a man with too much.'

He crossed his legs over tightly and leaned against the arm of the couch as though he was being squeezed into the corner by his memories. I could see above his elegant shoes and thin socks, a silvery, hairless shin. He settled himself, and talked, not about Miller or Lundt, but about imagination.

6

Years ago (he was still a reporter), he knew a man who was the epitome of the true man of action, a war hero. This man could be persuaded, with difficulty, for he was modest, to tell about his time as a soldier, before he inhaled mustard gas in the trenches on a winter dawn. He remembered everything: the grey mud of no-man's land, the stumps of trees, the rats, the aching guts, the fear, the obscene litter of the dead. JP had heard this man talk and had seen old soldiers weep silently as they listened.

One night, on his way home from an assignment, JP went into a pub in another town, and saw the same man at a corner table, surrounded by a group of intent listeners. JP bought a glass of beer and joined them. He was looking forward to hearing about those nightmare battlefields again. But this time the man was not talking about trench warfare. He was telling how a ship, the *Vaunted*, with a crew of six hundred, was torpedoed one night in winter. He said that he himself was one of those who had survived the blast and staggered half-clothed out of a sudden furnace onto the tilted deck. They could feel the ship being sucked down as they leaped into the numbing sea. With a few shipmates, he managed to climb onto a wooden raft, and spent three days on it, with one man after the other dying of cold and despair.

At that point, the man noticed JP standing listening. He paused, then carried on. He said that, in the end, only two of them were rescued from the raft, in such bad condition they were never able to return to sea. Their war was over.

JP finished his drink and left. He found out, later, that because of a bad heart, the man had been excluded from service in the war. But he could tell his imaginary experiences so well, he was more convincing than those who had actually been there.

'He was a liar,' said JP, 'and yet the real men of action did not betray him.'

He was silent for a long time, watching me closely. I knew I must respond in some way. So I tried to smile, by making the skin tighten around my jaws and my eyes. He seemed satisfied with my effort, and returned to the story of Lundt.

7

The office is lit only by his desk light. The door is slightly ajar. He sits upright, the black pistol on his desk, waiting. Two minutes to eight. He hears the squeal of hinges at the far end of the corridor, the thud of a door, the snap of leather soles on the tiled floor. He picks up the phone and dials. He breathes into it:

'Police? My name's Lundt. A man's outside my office with a gun. At City Hall. Please come, right now.'

He puts down the receiver. The footsteps in the corridor stop outside the door. His heart does not pound as much as he had feared. His hands do not shake. He knows he will have the strength. He desires nothing more in life now than to see the face of the man who will die.

He picks up the pistol with his handkerchief and presses the end of the cool barrel against his ear. He hears the tap on the door. He takes one last, deep breath:

'Come in!'

The door swings further ajar.

'Is everything okay, Mr Lundt? You're here late to- . . .'

The wrong voice precedes the wrong face. It is Tomson, the janitor, who stands at the door, shocked.

He looks back at him. Just for a moment. Then he squeezes the trigger.

8

'Did I mention,' said JP, 'that as my father grew older, he was always trying to show me that the world made sense, pointing out patterns, anything that would indicate order. He was afraid I might grow up to be a cynic. I couldn't understand his fear. Some men do not need to search for order, they are overwhelmed by it, everywhere they turn. They feel as though they're in a prison where each moment of the day is planned, every action overseen. They hunger for the smallest particles of chaos, for things that do not fit. But everything always fits, in the end.'

He said this in a light tone, but I thought I detected a touch of self-pity that made the silvery voice squeak slightly, in need of oil. After a moment, he went on with the story of Lundt.

'*The Post* sent me over to City Hall about nine o'clock that night. It was snowing heavily. The building was in a commotion. The police let me upstairs to take a look so that I could make an accurate report. The force of the shot had knocked Lundt's body over against the wall. The gun was lying near him, and a handkerchief. There was blood on the walls and the floor. I had to go right back outside for some air. I was very young then.' It was hard to believe JP had ever been young.

Two police officers, he discovered, had answered Lundt's emergency call and arrived at City Hall just after eight, at the same time as Jack Miller, all three of them like latecomers to a party. They all heard the shot, and ran up to Lundt's office. Tomson the janitor was standing at the door.

The police immediately arrested him, presuming he was the killer, the one Lundt had phoned about. Tomson said he was no killer, he was just doing his usual evening rounds and had noticed Lundt's office light. He opened the door and saw the poor man with a pistol at his head, and watched him shoot himself.

As for Miller, he said he had come in answer to Lundt's telephone call earlier. He would have been a few minutes sooner, but he'd walked across to the tobacco shop to buy a cigar.

Tomson was released next morning. By then, the letters about the debt had been found in Lundt's office, and several people had received those other, ominous notes.

It was all very strange. The police interrogated Miller again. He insisted he knew Lundt only as an employee, he certainly hadn't lent him any money, and he'd neither written any letters to him, nor received any, for that matter. As for the Beretta with his prints all over it, he had no idea how Lundt came to have it. The police were puzzled. Miller's own lawyer assured him that if he'd arrived at City Hall a little earlier that night, he might well be facing hanging, so much incriminating evidence pointed to him.

So far as the police were concerned, the matter was closed. Lundt was dead, a clear-cut case of suicide. The coroner speculated that Lundt had most likely intended to kill Miller and plead self-defence. When he saw Tomson, not Miller at the door, he knew his scheme had failed. He had set too many elements in motion, what with the theft of the Beretta, the letters, the final phone call to the police. He could not face the consequences, and shot himself.

9

'But,' said JP, 'why did he want to kill Miller in the first place? That was what interested me. Lundt was such an unlikely would-be murderer. I talked to Miller about it once or twice, but he was no help. By the end of the week, he'd put Lundt out of his mind. All he cared about was his election chances.'

It took JP nothing more than a conversation with Lundt's landlady, an elderly widow, to discover that he hated Miller. Lundt had often spoken to her about his supervisor's success with women. He became especially bitter when Miller seduced one young woman in particular, a new secretary at City Hall. Lundt secretly adored her. So when Miller, after a few weeks, cast her aside in his usual way, it was the last straw. Lundt told his landlady, several times, he'd gladly die to see justice done.

JP rearranged his limbs on the couch. From time to time as he talked, he would pat his silver hair in place, an unconscious vanity. I wondered if he himself had once been a ladies' man.

'I think the coroner was only half-right about Lundt's reason for killing himself.' JP said.

In JP's view, Lundt was afraid, most of all, that everyone would know he was nothing but a romantic misfit.

'To avenge someone implies great intimacy,' said JP. 'Lundt had gone to such lengths for the sake of a woman who would probably have loathed him, if she had ever noticed him. He realized the futility of his gesture in that final moment, and chose death.'

10

JP was motionless, watching me from behind a faint odour of shaving lotion. All at once, I realized he was waiting for me to say something. So for the first time since he began his story, I spoke.

'But according to Tomson, Lundt already had the pistol at his own head when he pushed the door open. How did he expect to shoot Miller after he'd shot himself?'

JP, smiling his sick lizard smile, congratulated me on asking the right question. As for the right answer, he could only speculate. Lundt, he said, was a moral man, a man with a conscience, quite incapable of killing anyone else. His landlady had told JP this several times, and insisted Lundt wouldn't hurt a fly.

'But he didn't mind if the state killed Miller,' said JP.

He was certain that Lundt's plan was to commit a reverse murder-suicide: from the start, he had always intended to shoot himself with Miller's Beretta, having arranged for the police to arrive immediately afterwards and catch Miller on the scene. Miller's lawyer was right, there was so much evidence against him he would surely have hanged. What judge would even have suspected that a man could be foolish enough to kill himself as a means of bringing about someone else's execution?

Nor did Lundt regard his proposed killing of himself, anyway, as suicide: he was too moral for that.

'He believed,' said JP, 'that he was simply executing himself, in advance, for his indirect murder of Miller. He was so certain his plan was foolproof and that Miller would hang. Then Tomson, the janitor, opened the door, and that was what turned his death into suicide.'

JP's mouth opened a little wider, and I saw his fine silvery teeth for the first time. He said, 'A month later, Miller won the election.'

11

The lizard cackled, then was silent, then spoke quite soberly:

'Lundt was a man to whom women were too important. I myself once had the same weakness, at a certain time of my life.'

I could see he was now confiding in me; that, after testing me with the story of Lundt, he was about to tell me something more personal.

When he was an adolescent, he said, he used to browse through the telephone directory and touch the names of women. That was the forerunner of the time, in his twenties, when he spent most of his energy in the pursuit of flesh-and-blood women. He was a man of many faces then, not out of hypocrisy, but because he didn't yet know for sure what kind of man he wanted to be.

I listened to him attentively now. Perhaps I sensed that something of peculiar interest to me might lie somewhere in his memory.

12

He said that during that period of his life (his late twenties) he began to live according to a theory he happened to have constructed for himself. It went like this: a truly well-balanced life will inevitably undergo abrupt alterations or deflections to counterbalance its moments of relative constancy. If life became too pleasing, the wise man would positively court his quota of pain; if his life became too secure, he would deliberately expose himself to danger.

Accordingly, JP would from time to time drive cars that were too fast for him; or he would climb cliff-faces too steep for a man like himself, who frequently stumbled on staircases; he would shoot rapids (he told no one he could not swim); and when, in the course of time, he became a war correspondent, he would expose himself needlessly to hostile bullets.

As for women. Once, at that time, he wooed a woman who was different from any other he had known. She frightened him a little, a woman who loved the night.

He licked his silver lips. This was what he wanted to tell me about.

The war was over, he said, his assignment in Europe ended. He was working for a newspaper in the city, settling down, when one of his friends happened to mention that a woman of some beauty had joined the evening typing pool. JP, ever on the look-out, took an article to the typists' office that night. He saw the woman.

She really was beautiful. He fell in love with her and made up his mind to have her.

That was the beginning of a strange affair. Sometimes she would respond to him with passion and energy, sometimes she would treat him with contempt. He could never entirely trust her, but he wanted her. He asked her to marry him, something he had never done before.

JP rose again stiffly from the sofa and poured us each a goblet of wine, a silver goblet. As he handed it to me, he said casually:

'She was from your part of the world. Some island. Her name was Rachel Mackenzie.'

I did not give myself away as I had at the Institute for the Lost. I stayed calm. I thought, Mackenzie is such a common name. Rachel is such a common name. I did not interrupt him. I did not ask him to proceed. I knew he would. If he expected me to say something, I disappointed him. He sipped the wine through silver lips, for a while, then put the goblet back down on the table, and began to remember his last meeting with the woman on a warm night in August . . .

13

. . . on a warm night in August, she decided to kill Rachel Mackenzie, for she could take no more. They had managed to get along together passably well for years; indeed, at times, she thought she could almost have loved Rachel.

But the end was inevitable, hope was as good as over when Rachel met this man, and decided after a few weeks to encourage him. Nothing would make her understand how foolish it was to bring another man into their lives, even as a diversion. The idea was intolerable. Rachel wept and tried to conciliate her, as she always did. But this time her pleading wouldn't work. This was the last straw, she would take no more.

He, whenever he came to the apartment, looked uncomfortable. He was so attracted to Rachel, nonetheless, that he kept coming back, no matter how awkward she made things.

She knew she herself was beautiful, just as beautiful in her own way as Rachel. But she was not the type men liked, no matter how much she forced herself to smile at them, no matter how hard she tried to camouflage her eyes.

Rachel, as on other occasions when she had a man, would be impatient with her.

'Just leave me alone. Why do you spend all your time watching me?'

'Do I?'

Rachel would occasionally plead with her, tears in her eyes: 'Please, tell me why. At least talk to me. I am the one who is not good with words.'

'Oh? Is that so?' she would invariably reply.

And listen to her sobbing.

On the night of the killing, the house smelt musty from the sun all day, and the sky outside was thundery. Rachel and the man had gone out for dinner, to celebrate something, any excuse to get out of the house, away from her, to be alone together. When they came home, Rachel, looking marvellous in her low-cut green dress, greeted her with that false smile she would put on when she was determined to have her way.

But she herself looked right back at her, not saying what she was thinking: Rachel, I loathe you, you've gone too far.

She watched, disgusted, as Rachel took him by the hand, neither of them paying any more attention to her, and led him into the bedroom. She pushed him back on the bed and lay on top of him, the two of them fully clothed, and kissed him, slipping her tongue into his mouth, running her hands over his body. She unbuttoned his shirt, pulled it from under him, and dropped it on the floor. She began kissing his neck, his white shoulders, nuzzling the sprinkle of reddish hairs on his white, sweaty chest.

They ignored her, though she was standing watching as she always did. She had seen Rachel operate so often before, she could forecast what she would do.

She would run her tongue along his chest, sipping at his tiny, man's nipples. She would undo his belt, as he breathed faster and faster. She would kneel, and pull his pants and his underpants slowly down over his knees, till they were shackles around his ankles. Then, slowly, looking at him looking at her adoringly, she would lie beside him and fondle him, and she would take him into her mouth till he was bursting with excitement.

He was hardly able to contain himself, begging for her, and she stood and began to undress herself, deliberately, letting him admire her.

Then Rachel turned to her, still watching.

'Do you want to?' she asked, sneering. 'Why don't you go ahead?' The old routine.

Rachel knew her only too well, that in spite of herself, she was roused, that she did, indeed, want him.

So she herself lay down on the bed, spreading herself to receive him. He hesitated at the sight of her, but then he climbed on top of her, his body slippery with sweat, and thrust at her for a few minutes with his eyes tight shut and, with a shudder, released himself into her. Smelling his sweat, she squirmed under him, milking every drop of him, leaving nothing for Rachel.

She decided, at that very moment, that she would kill the bitch before the night was over.

After a while, he arose, looking a little embarrassed, and dressed hurriedly. He kissed Rachel goodbye, saying he would phone her tomorrow. And left.

She herself went to the bathroom to sponge away his sweat and his semen. She preened herself in the mirror, stretched her arms luxuriously, aware Rachel was looking. She combed back her hair, noticed how blue her eyes were, bluer than ever tonight.

Then she slid open the right-hand drawer. She could see the tip of the knife protruding. She made no attempt to disguise her action even though Rachel was now watching her intently. Her fingers caressed the point, brushed along the blade till they felt the handle of the bread knife that had lain there so long for just such a night as this. She was aware of the beating of her heart.

She raised the knife in the air, looking directly at Rachel. Those eyes did not flinch. She had expected to see terror in them. Why was she not pleading, instead of watching her raised hand, long fingered, the nails scarlet, a gold ring on the middle finger?

And now Rachel began taunting her, laughing at her, come on, do it, do it, why don't you do it?

Till she herself could stand it no more. Inflamed with anger, shouting her contempt, she hacked once with the knife at the white, naked throat, ripping apart the soft carotid artery.

As she herself lay on the cool, white-tiled floor, the blood bubbling out of her throat and her mouth, relief filled all of her being. She had heard Rachel's cry of fear as the knife struck. She had glimpsed, as she fell, the bread knife at her neck, the spout of blood. For the first time in too many years, her own world was singular and full of light. At long last, she really was herself, alone, and at peace.

14

JP came to her apartment the next night, a little anxiously, for his telephone calls had not been answered. He had warned her about the dangers of living alone, and she had laughed.

He opened the apartment door with his duplicate key.

Rachel's body was fastened to the white-tiled bathroom floor by a stalagmite of blood, and there were splashes of blood on the mirror and the counter. The knife was in her hand, and he had no doubt it was suicide. He looked around the apartment before calling the police. In the perfumed drawer of her desk he found sheets of paper with circular shapes on them. At first glance, he thought they were tremulous drawings of mad eyes. Or they might have been whirlpools or coils of rope. But then he saw that the marks were, in fact, thin spirals of her tiny handwriting. On some of them, she had begun her writing in the centre of the page and continued in concentric form till she reached the edges. Conversely, on some of the others, she had started writing at the edge and gradually narrowed the spiral till she reached the centre. Some were clockwise, some anti-clockwise. On all of the sheets, the same words were written, either from the edges in, or from the centres out, 'weperisheachaloneweperisheachaloneweperish . . .'

15

Later, said JP, the police found some notebooks of hers. They too were full of her spirals. Except on one page, where she had written that, for years, she'd had sex with men in order to become pregnant. She'd aborted the foetuses and preserved them in jars of formaldehyde. Of course, no such jars were found.

Both JP and the police considered the idea to be nothing but the fantasy of a poor, demented woman. Aside from certain moments (often, JP admitted, the most intimate of moments) when her eyes would become distant, she was a quiet, beautiful woman. He saw no need to tell the police that it was because he was a little afraid of her that he had pursued her in the first place.

I sat watching and listening as JP leaned his head back on the sofa, and put his silvery hand to his mouth to cover a yawn, a snake's yawn.

'I was surprised I did not feel very sad at her death,'

he said. 'Like Lundt's, it seemed to me more of a tidying up of loose ends than the annihilation of a life.'

He talked on like this for some time, the old man, JP. He looked very old, I could see he had grown tired. The scent of his shaving lotion (a fine, silvery scent) was stronger now in proportion as his energy weakened. The time was right for a question.

'Did she have some kind of abdominal scar?' I asked.

He looked at me, curious. But he was too worn out by his memories, as I had hoped, to inquire about the reason for my interest.

'Not that I ever noticed.'

One more thing I needed to ask.

'Have you ever heard of Doctor Yerdeli, the Director of the Institute for the Lost?'

I was watching very carefully. But he might have been on his guard now, too. Certainly, that reptile face did not betray him in any way.

'No.'

I had to be satisfied with that. He was not a man who would tolerate inquisitions. So I convinced myself that he had not told me about the death of Rachel Mackenzie to elicit some reaction from me, or make me commit myself. He seemed much too self-interested for that, and too tired now to care. Though perhaps if I had been a woman, he would not have allowed his tiredness to show. He might even have shown some interest in me, and asked about my own life.

As I left, he wound his elegant, thin legs together and lay back on the couch. The tubular collar of his silk

polo-neck sweater swallowed his scrawny neck and part
of his chin. Lying down like that, there was no hiding
the thinness of the hair on his oval head. It made me think
of a tarnished silver egg disappearing into the throat of
a misshapen snake.

16

I was glad to be alone in my car, driving back to the
city. I had plenty of time to wonder if, in a world
of so many people, I had actually chanced on another
of those four Patagonian Mackenzies. I thought, it's
too much of a coincidence, too uncalled for. I had
seen no conniving gleam in the silver eye of JP when
he spoke about Rachel, no hint that he and Doctor
Yerdeli were conspiring; but when you stumble on
too many coincidences, or on unexpected coincidences,
or on coincidences you have no right to expect, it
is natural to look for some sort of a joke, or for a
joker. In the end, I concluded that if Rachel Mackenzie
was a member of the Patagonian Mackenzies, I had
found out about her by an incomprehensible stroke
of chance. I wasn't sure I should be too happy about
that.

17

That night, in a small restaurant near my apartment, as Helen and I were drinking brandy after dinner, I asked her about her day and told her about mine. I had saved it till then, organizing the details in my mind all the way home in the car and through the earlier part of the evening. I sniffed the brandy for a while, then I told her about JP and about Gerald Lundt's attempted crime. I told her about JP's affair with a woman called Rachel Mackenzie (I noticed with satisfaction Helen's surprise at the name), her delusions, and her death. I became a little poetic, from the brandy or from talking too much.

'JP told me all this down there in his country house. Through his long front window I could see soft hills, green fields, and blue sky. From time to time, one of those black horse-drawn carriages would go pecking along. There was a symmetry between them and JP's recollections that made me shudder.'

Helen reacted to everything I told her just the way I had hoped: with curiosity, surprise, sadness. She had roller-coasted through these states, just as I had.

I remembered something else JP had said. A question really. He had wondered if he himself, by falling in love with Rachel Mackenzie, must take partial responsibility for her death. He wondered if love violates certain people: they have to reveal too much about themselves, they feel so full of holes and weaknesses, they can't live any more.

I told Helen I had not been able to think of anything to say in response. She looked at me and pressed my arm:

'Ezra, I think he's right, in a way. But there's no avoiding it. The more people love each other, the more they violate each other. They sweat and wrestle and howl and penetrate each other, and want to know all about each other. No privacy is permitted. They give each other the third degree. So he's right. But if lovers don't violate each other, love dies.'

I laughed and said I'd like to test her theory: at least, the sweating, wrestling, howling, penetrating part of it. Just to see if I agreed. So we left the restaurant, and went home to bed, and tested it. And afterwards, before we fell asleep, I told her, yes, the theory was a good one.

18

Later that week, I wrote to Donald Cromarty. In my letter, I told him I had now come across another Mackenzie, named Rachel, and gave him the details. As I was writing, I realized I had still not told Helen that I had enlisted his help. I think I kept it to myself because I knew, instinctively, she would have disapproved. And perhaps if I had been less willing to confide in him, I would never have had to face him, in the end, at the Paradise Motel.

In my letter, I told him everything. I made it clear I was no surer this Rachel could be a member of the Patagonian Mackenzies than the Amos Mackenzie I had written him about earlier. Then I asked what progress he was making with his inquiries into my grandfather Daniel Stevenson's story. I let him know I was aware of the obstacles before him: the destruction of archives in the war; the depopulation of many of the islands; the discretion, almost amounting to deceit, of news reporting in that era.

I encouraged him, flattered him, thanked him. I hoped he would let me know what he had found when I returned from my next journey. For I was already preparing to go south.

Part Four

ESTHER

Esther Mackenzie was sent, at the same time as her younger sister, Rachel, to St Fiona's orphanage, near the Border. She was, by thirteen, a heavily built girl with black hair who had never seen herself naked. The day the first blood stained her underwear, she felt immediate sorrow for all the other girls, and ceased to believe in God (though she kept that a secret from the Sisters of the Holy Order of Correction).

She was an excellent mimic, but she displayed this gift to no one. She would go down to a little hollow in the fields near the orphanage and contort her body to simulate the mannerisms of others, particularly of Sister Marie Jerome, a small French nun with rickets, who was in charge of discipline. But she stopped going there after finding, one day, at the bottom of the hollow, a little image made of mud. It had bent legs, and was draped in a black cloth. The image had been pierced with sharp twigs. From then on, Esther Mackenzie stopped her mimicry, and trained herself to take all emotion out of her voice, so that everything she said was as inflectionless as the written word.

The other orphans sought her friendship because of her plain appearance, and would have liked her more if she had confided in them. But she preferred the company of the animals at the orphanage farm, because they asked her no questions.

By the time she finally left the orphanage, the thought of dying in that cold, Border country appalled her. She worked as a waitress for some months, then, in the last year of the war, spent a year with the Red Cross. She often watched surgery, marvelling at the body's capacity to endure bullets and scalpels. She had few sexual experiences, nor did she desire them much, though she had vivid sexual dreams. Her thick body, her monotonous voice disguised her mind. One morning she failed to appear at the hospital. She had taken passage on a ship bound south-west, for the tropics. She met her family only once, after leaving the orphanage.

Notebook, A. McGAW

1

Helen, out of a sense of obligation, had to go on a trip north for a couple of months to visit her family, so I, at a loose end, went south. A friend had suggested the idea. He had travelled in the region a few years before, in the course of exploring one of his cases (he was a policeman), and thought I would find the experience interesting.

So, a week later, I was in the tropical south. I took a room in a hotel in Xtecal, a village where the jungle meets the sea, about a hundred miles south of the main provincial city. Each mile, I found out, was a year's journey back in time. As for the village, it was shrinking. Not long ago, it had been a town; before that, a city. But this withering away seemed to concern no one who lived there. Perhaps the villagers shared the spirit of the ancient peoples who had settled that country, and who had built nothing to last. It was said that their greatest edifices were made to endure only the length of the builders' lives. At the end of that time, builders and buildings were buried, and new structures rose on top of them.

To trace the original, overgrown streets and the ruins of much of Xtecal would have challenged a crypto-grapher's skill. In the part that was still inhabited, clans

137

of rats and domestic pigs disputed the right of way with the human population. Only a few hundred people persisted in living here, witnessing daily the powers of nature's bailiff, the jungle, as it reclaimed its rightful property.

The Plazacar Hotel, in which I took a room, was a relic of Xtecal's more recent glory days. It was a palace gone to seed, smelling of decay, with a wide, grass-roofed patio in need of repair. The owners lived far away, in the provincial capital, but they kept the hotel open. I suppose they felt that just as Xtecal had mysteriously declined, so it might as mysteriously resurrect and achieve its former glory.

The supreme attraction of the Plazacar, according to the desk-clerk, was its portable beach bar, thirty feet of polished mahogany that was carried each day onto the hotel's private beach. The bar was set up in the middle of the beach. If it had been of regular height, it would have blocked the view of sunbathers, but it was only a foot or two tall, and lay on the sand like a long coffin. The bartender, too, and the waiter were each no more than three feet tall.

This waiter, Gilberto, when I got to know him, told me that for generations his family had produced a tiny waiter to serve at the Plazacar. He himself, to carry on the tradition, had married the shortest girl in Xtecal. But she was four feet tall, and, unfortunately, their son had taken after the mother. I used to meet Gilberto in the street from time to time, with his son, who was then seven years old and already a head taller than his father. The boy had a birthmark in the shape of a perfect triangle of jet-black skin around his right eye.

Every night, if the rain stayed away, dinner was served on the hotel patio. Two local men, who accompanied themselves on worn guitars, would entertain the diners with sad ballads. The tenor, a very ugly man, had a long wart-covered nose and an angelic voice. He always stood well away from the light. Gilberto told me that sensitive guests, in former years, had complained of the presence of that nose when they were eating. The sight of it, I must confess, did have a damping effect on the appetite.

2

During my stay in Xtecal, I followed a routine: I would spend much of each day reading, sipping the local rum. Then, about four in the afternoon, I would defy the sun and go for long walks down the beach. Sometimes, in fact, I walked so far, darkness would creep up behind me, and the thick jungle would wedge me towards the sea. On those days, I would have to hurry back at a trot towards the distant lights of my sanctuary, Xtecal.

Those were my usual habits. But one morning, after a

surprise storm had howled all night, I went on my walk early. The shore was a chaos of beer bottles, broken palm fronds, detergent containers, putrid fish, and pieces of styrofoam wrapped in seaweed.

I was passing the last huts at the edge of the village, when I saw a man coming along the beach towards me, not in a straight line but weaving, his head down, as though he was hypnotized by the litter on the beach. But nearer, I saw he was drunk, that he was not a native, and that he had seen me.

I would have avoided him, but there was no place to go except into the jungle or the water. So I tried not to see him, to make my face a blank wall to him. But he was not to be put off, and as he came nearer, he greeted me in fisherman's Spanish: 'Buena dia!' And I could not ignore him.

He was a man in his late sixties, perhaps, with a long, wiry body, and a bush of thick grey hair. A labyrinth of old scars and age wrinkles bracketed his eyes. The half-empty bottle of rum in his left hand oiled his walk.

He stood in my path, now, swaying, but his blue eyes were steadier than mine. He held out his bottle, a sociable gesture. I refused it as politely as I could. The edges of his words had been smoothed by the rum. But he seemed good-humoured and harmless, and after a few minutes, I was glad to stand and talk to him, or listen to him talk.

3

That was my first meeting with Pablo Renowsky. Nothing could have been more accidental, I would say. I had travelled south on a whim. I had come by pure chance to this village of Xtecal, a name chosen arbitrarily from a tourist guidebook. I had met him because there had been an unseasonable storm, and because that morning, the only morning in my whole stay, I walked early rather than late.

His name was really Paul, but the villagers called him Pablo or Pablito. They enjoyed treating him as the drunken gringo, and he did not seem to mind. I never did see him really drunk; his speech was slurred, but not only by rum as I had first thought. Boxing was the main cause. He had been a professional boxer for twenty years. In addition to the neanderthal scar tissue above his eyes, a pink cauliflower had sprouted in place of his left ear. But when he spoke, it was as though the door to a ruined mansion swung open, and revealed elegant furniture and curious paintings. For Pablo Renowsky was an intellectual boxer. He was, with his inquisitive, discreet attitude, a scholar: a scholar with a deviated septum which he often wiped with his thumb as he talked.

His ramshackle hut on the beach, where I spent several afternoons after our first meeting, was full of books, all of them well read by him. Many of them now served mainly as homes for families of ants, and scorpions, and

141

tarantulas. Still, out of a feeling of gratitude towards his books, he kept them till they rotted or were eaten.

He talked quite a lot about his past, but never romantically, never boasting about his boxing days (he had been a jabber, not a big puncher). His life story was not, he felt, unusual: he once had strict farmer-parents; he resolved to run away from home; he lived on the streets; he discovered he had a talent for boxing, and could make a living at it; he served an apprenticeship, during which he was punched around too many times, till he learnt what he could do and what he couldn't. He had entered a world he had never known existed, whose inhabitants regarded gonorrhoea and head colds as equally minor, and who settled trivial quarrels in back alleys, wordlessly, with knives.

Pablo told me about his boxing life with its rituals of disrobing, the use of oils and massage; the embraces and fondlings in the ring; the bruises, the explosive releases; the climaxes in unconsciousness, or even in death.

He spoke, too, of the women he had known, many of them tough camp followers. But one or two were good women, the best. He showed me a faded photograph of the woman he had married. I could not decipher her features. She had died, not long after the wedding, he said sadly.

In the course of his travels, he read and read. Sometimes his trainer would rebuke him for reading as he lay in the liniment-smelling dressing-room just before a fight, when he should have been concentrating on the battle to come. But Pablo felt his reading and his boxing complemented each other. Nothing was more effective, he assured me, for establishing the relationship between essence and existence than the pain a straight left to the nose could give.

As he grew older, his wily legs let him down, and he began to lose easy fights. So he made up his mind to come down here and live out the rest of his life. He had saved enough money to survive comfortably in this place, and though it was no Eden, he felt better than when he was a target by profession. He bought this hut on the beach and settled down, thinking he might write about his experiences. But in that, he had never succeeded.

Was it possible, he wondered, his blue eyes fixing mine, that all the words in his brain had been pounded out of shape by too many punches, so he could no longer make them fit his life? Or (he looked at me hopefully), did I know if it was the case with words, that they never did fit anyway? But if that were so, how would anyone understand for sure what anyone else was saying?

He had tried learning Spanish, thinking that perhaps a fresh language was what he needed. But the foreign words made him feel stiff, constrained, like a jungle animal that must from now on travel only by maps.

Some years ago, he said, while he was asleep, he had *dreamt* an entire novel: dreamt that he had sweated it out of himself for months, or maybe years; then had polished it; that it was published; that it was admired by some readers, reviled by others. He dreamt all this in just a few minutes one night. Perhaps, he said, having experienced so vividly in a dream everything a writer goes through, his need to write an actual book had been satisfied? Perhaps that was why he preferred now to read, and to remember?

4

In his hut, as he sat drinking his rum, he would at times switch to his metaphysical concerns, some of which were disconcerting. For example, he might say:

'I wonder why it is that parents don't murder their children?' He could not understand why a mother, especially, did not hate the child who sucked her dry. Surely a mother's restraint was one of the great miracles.

Another time, he told me how, whenever he went to a zoo, the sight of visitors laughing derisively at the monkeys always made him sad. It was tempting to say the people were really laughing at themselves, because the monkeys were the next nearest things to human beings and, therefore, fit only to be laughed at. But Pablo wondered if they weren't, rather, laughing at innocence. He didn't go to zoos any more.

'When you know what innocence is,' he said, 'you know that you yourself are no longer innocent. Isn't that so?'

I could see he was anxious about my opinion on this, so I said that the problem was certainly worth thinking about.

During those afternoons in his hut, he talked mainly about the old days in Xtecal, when he first arrived. Then, newcomers always noticed, right in the middle of the town square, next to the bandstand, the bullet-pocked wall with its white-painted lines on the ground: the official execution area. A town where the symbols of law and order were so prominent was bound to prosper. And it had.

But that was long ago. Xtecal had declined, reminding him of many broken-down boxers he had known, seedy but still worthy of respect for their pasts.

In this way, Pablo Renowsky would speculate, ask his questions, and reminisce. Of all the conversations I had with him, however, I remember best the story of his visit to one of the most notable places in the old Xtecal, a bar called La Cueva, now completely returned to the jungle. Pablo thumbed his nose more vigorously than usual as he thought back to the times he went there. It was, he said, one place he could never forget.

5

I wasn't the only gringo who lived here back then. There were a few others, mainly on the run for smuggling arms or drugs. I became friendly with one of them, and one night he came to my hut. Pablo, he said, it's about time you saw the real culture here.

So I went out with him.

We didn't have to go very far, just a half-mile walk through the town, towards the jungle. The jungle's grown back in now, like a scab over a wound. But at that time, the town was a big place, and it was eerie to walk through it at night. There were no street lamps. The main street was full of the shapes of people, hundreds of them, and you could hear voices from all the shops and cafés and houses. The insides of the buildings were lit by candles or hurricane lamps. It was easy to imagine that this was the way it must have been, for hundreds of years, and the voices must have sounded the same then, in the dark.

We came to the edge of the jungle and walked for a while along a gloomy path with big trees on all sides. There was no moon. It was after nine o'clock, and you could hear the jungle animals crashing and rustling in the bushes. I was always afraid, at that time, of standing on a snake. But never mind snakes, there were always plenty of mosquitoes biting at your ankles, even though the townspeople used to burn bushes to keep them down. I don't know what was worse, the mosquitoes or the smell of that smoke.

Up ahead, I could see lights, and hear guitars. There was a big grass-roofed building. When we reached it, I could read the sign outside. It said La Cueva. A woman of about fifty was standing at the bamboo gate, greeting everyone who went in. She was a gringo, too, I could see that right away. She was heavily built, but in a balanced kind of a way: I mean, the weight hadn't sunk into the bottom half of her yet. Her eyes were brown and her skin was brown, but she was a gringo, all right. She was speaking in Spanish, but as we came out of the dark, she saw my friend, and she switched to English. She knew him from before.

He introduced us: Pablo, this is the Senora, she owns the place.

That was the first time I met her, but I met her often after that. I liked her, and I liked her husband, Delio, when I met him later. I don't know what kind of life she had before ending up in this town, owning a place like La Cueva. You didn't ask that kind of thing in those days. But there was a look in her eyes I often saw in old boxers that made me feel she'd seen a lot. Delio was a professional carnival performer. They'd met in some other little jungle town, twenty years before, and hit it off. He was younger than the Senora, maybe ten years younger. Her voice was very monotonous, as though she'd had an operation on it: she played on one note all the time. They were two of the most contented people you could ever meet, a rare thing.

But on the first night, all I saw was a solidly build gringo woman who was the owner of this seedy bar at the edge of the jungle.

The inside of La Cueva was full of cigarette smoke and the smell of kerosene lamps and sweat. The main floor had a bar and about fifty tables with people at them. There was a wooden guard-rail along one side, where the ground fell away to a deep grotto, and a rickety wooden stair led down there. From the guard-rail, I could see tables down in the grotto too, and behind them an illuminated stage against a background of rock. On the main floor, where we were, a dozen half-naked women were looking after about sixty or seventy male customers. Some of the women were pretty, but most of them had sagging breasts, or big bellies, or

147

no teeth. The men they were serving drinks to weren't much to look at, either. They seemed to have pot-bellies or no backsides. But they were drunk, that was for sure. There was some kind of gallery above the bar. You could see a row of bamboo cubicles with ragged curtains on them. Some of the women would take men up there, by a side-stair.

My friend had brought me here for the floor show, so we found two seats by the guard-rail round the crater. The show was held on the stage down there. The tables in that pit were packed with drunks. We didn't have long to wait.

The show began with a mad-looking Indian woman coming out on the stage from behind some boulders, carrying a bag over her shoulder. When she put the bag down in the spotlight, we could see that it wasn't a bag at all, it was a live baby, with no head. And no arms or legs. It had a mouth and eyes set into a little mound where its neck should have been. The woman began to feed it milk and husks, and we could hear the slurping noise, and see the little eyes rolling. The woman didn't do anything else, just feed her baby. Most of the audience wasn't paying any attention. As my friend said, you could see this kind of thing in the streets any day, you didn't have to come to La Cueva.

The next act was a repeat, but it was by popular demand. The spectators were interested this time. A nervous-looking old man came on stage, walking with a limp, holding a cloth round his body. He dropped the cloth, and everybody laughed. He had no trousers on, and the cloth had hidden a scrotum that was as big as an elephant's. It was hanging down to his knees, like a watermelon, with a little stub of a penis at the top. The audience were laughing and shouting to him, and the old man stood there, quite happy.

My friend had heard about this case. The old man had developed a hernia years ago, and couldn't afford to have it fixed. His intestine had slipped down into his scrotum, more and more, till the bag was full and weighed nearly thirty pounds. He had earned enough money now to have it fixed, and in fact the doctor had warned him it might burst any day. But the old man said if he had it fixed now, they wouldn't want to see him on stage any more, so he wouldn't hear of it.

After the old man, the rest of the acts were the kind of sex acts you could see in a lot of taverns at that time: snakes crawling in and out of vaginas; men and women having sex with dogs and mules; a crazy thin man with a penis like a long twig, poking it into the eye hole of a one-eyed woman; a fat man, standing on a stool, trying to make love to a Brahmin cow. The cow didn't seem to mind, but all at once, it lifted its tail and emptied its bowels all over his legs. The audience thought that was funny, even if the fat man didn't.

That was a typical kind of mid-week show at La Cueva. But you wouldn't dream of comparing it with one of Delio's performances. No, not in any way.

6

Delio and the Senora owned the first car ever seen down here. She told me how they got it. They had to have it brought in by boat, for there wasn't a single passable road outside the limits of Xtecal. Even the town roads were awful. They were meant mainly for walking or for mules. The car was big and well sprung. I don't know how they managed to keep it running, what with the heat and the rot. The only driving they did was up and down the main street, once a day. That was their only affectation, though they were rich, for Xtecal.

For twenty years, Delio had been one of the best-known carnival performers in this whole state. The first time I saw his act, I knew that what I went through in the ring was nothing at all. He was an *agujado*: once a month, for twenty years, he had made a living by having his body pierced with skewers. Not just through the flesh: amateurs could do that. The really famous *agujados* had the skewers run right through their bodies from front to back or from side to side.

That was how Delio met the senora. He needed a new assistant to insert the skewers, and she volunteered for the job. The assistants were called *agujereadores*, and were just as important as the *agujados*. Take the Senora: if she was no good, if she made a single mistake, she could kill him. She had to slide those skewers (*agujas*, they called them) into his body with dead aim, so that they missed the vital organs. Often she had only fractions of an inch to work with. She needed a cool head, a steady hand, and marvellous accuracy. She must have learnt somewhere about the internal structure of a man's body. She had to make sure the skewers went in and came out by pre-set paths, without any deviation. The experts used to say an *agujado*'s body was his private minefield. There was only one safe path through it, and only his personal *agujereador* knew the way.

Delio was not the only *agujado* in the world. Every major carnival had one. But what made his act better known than all the others was this: he'd made it into a competition. Over the years, he'd gradually increased the number of skewers that went into his body. Every year, he'd go for a new personal record, and announce in advance that he was going to try. Big audiences, a lot of them down from the city, came to these major performances, and there was a lot of gambling on the outcome. People used to bet on how many skewers he'd be able to accept; or whether he'd set a new record; or whether he'd die before reaching his previous mark; or whether his *agujereador*, the Senora, would make a fatal slip and kill him.

Most *agujados* could take ten or at most fifteen skewers. Some of the best of them had even challenged Delio, but given up or died in the attempt to compete with him. He was so successful, some people who didn't like him spread rumours that he'd bribed the *agujereadores* of his rivals or arranged to have their *agujas* poisoned. But no

151

one really believed the rumours. Delio was the greatest of them all, and proved it every time he performed. For Delio, ten skewers was just a warm-up. His record was twenty-five. And he had promised he would go higher before he retired.

There was a lot of gambling at these performances, but it was always kept discreet. That was part of the business, and both Delio and the Senora knew it went on. They knew their audiences were only human.

After a performance, the Senora would become Delio's nurse for a while, watching over him and tending his wounds so that they wouldn't fester, especially in the rainy season when everything rotted. Between monthly performances, he was wrapped in bandages most of the time, and there was always pus flowing from somewhere in his body.

I saw his final performance. He had announced a month before that he was going for his last record: twenty-six skewers, and then he'd retire for good. So, on that night, La Cueva was packed. My friend and I could hardly find a place to stand. The mayor was there, and the whole police department, and the lawyer-cum-dentist-cum-doctor, and the priest (he had to sit on his own, in the shadows: the church didn't approve of *agujados*). There had been the usual debate about which angles were the best for spectators: most preferred a side view, to see the entry and exit of the skewers; others like to look over the *agujereador*'s shoulder, to watch the placement. Others felt it was only important to see the exit of the skewers; they said that you could only judge how good an *agujereador* was if you could see how accurately the points came through.

7

A hush descends as the small man with deep brown eyes walks onto the stage, wearing a brief loincloth. She follows him, solid and serene. She straps him to the *estaca*, a post set up on the stage especially for the purpose. He stands sideways to the audience. The bindings are tight, so that he will remain steady during the performance. His slight body is marked by the stigmata of twenty years.

The woman, dressed in black, asks him if he is ready to receive the first skewer. He nods his head. She turns to the table that stands beside the *estaca*. A white cloth is laden with two-foot-long bone-handled skewers that glint in the light. She chooses one, turns and surveys the man's body the way a painter assesses a canvas. She places the point of the skewer at a scar just below his ribs, then thrusts smoothly till the skewer emerges through a corresponding scar in his back. La Cueva is silent enough for devotees to hear the swish of the skewer as it passes through the *agujado*'s body.

The man smiles. All is well. The woman continues with her task, sliding one skewer after another through the well-travelled passageways in his pale body. He begins to resemble a living statue of the patron of the *agujados*, Saint Sebastian.

After the insertion of the tenth skewer, the woman pauses to allow the customary applause.

The skewering begins again: fifteen, twenty. Another pause, another round of applause.

The tension is high. Twenty-one skewers. Twenty-two. Twenty-three. Twenty-four. The woman's aim is unerring, the man's flesh swallows the steel, blood drools from the tiny mouths in his belly and his back. He looks strong, he exults in his mastery of the skewers.

She slides the twenty-fifth skewer into him, equalling his old record. A roar of applause fills La Cueva. Now the woman looks at him, this tree of flesh that sprouts branches of steel.

She formally asks, as an *agujereador* must, if he will accept one more skewer. He, as the *agujado* must, formally asks her if she thinks his body will bear it. The woman looks to the audience for a moment, as though hoping they will tell her to stop. But this too is a formality. It is for this final skewer they have come to La Cueva.

She picks up the twenty-sixth skewer. She holds it delicately, her solid body steady as a rock in the grotto. She has dreamt this thrust a thousand times. The skewer will enter the man's body just below the bag of the stomach, it will slide swiftly through the space above the intestinal coil, and will exit on the left side of the fifteenth vertebra of the spine.

The woman places the point against the unbroken skin.

She concentrates, like an archer willing a bull's eye. The man braces his body, closes his eyes. She thrusts. She sees the brief indentation in the flesh, she feels, without seeing, the swift passage, the point emerge unresisting, the tiny volcano of split flesh in his back, the trickle of blood.

The man is motionless. Then, slowly, he opens his eyes, and smiles at the woman. She smiles back. The audience roars its approval, a roar that crashes all round the grotto, all round the jungle outside.

But the man's head jerks suddenly back, his body convulses like a snake's. His eyes roll upwards, his head sags to his chest.

The woman snatches skewers out of the limp body, dropping them, glinting, to the ground. Spectators help her unfasten the straps. They lay the body on the stage floor like a withered parchment, and contemplate its bloody message.

8

During the uproar, my friend said to me, Pablo, it's too late for a doctor now. He was right. The lawyer-dentist-doctor was one of the first down onto the stage. He was there partly for that kind of emergency. But Delio was dead. There wasn't a breath left in him. He was lying in the grotto of La Cueva, in front of five hundred people, dead.

It was a sad business, though a lot of hard-headed gamblers made a profit out of his death. They say *agujados* always push their luck too far, in the end, and the gamblers are bound to win eventually. But even they were sorry. My friend said, Pablo, it's too bad: the fear we all eat every day tastes a little more bitter after a man like Delio dies.

As for the Senora, she wasn't the kind of woman it's easy to console. You always felt that she knew more about life and death than most of us ever would, so what could you say to her? For myself, I said nothing and hoped she understood.

9

Pablo Renowsky had gone this far in his recollections, and I still hadn't made the connection. Perhaps I was too carried away. Even the fact that he had said more than once that the Senora was a gringo hadn't made much of an impression: gringo women were no rarer here at that time than gringo men. No, it took his next words: 'She had an accent like yours.'

Immediately, I advanced from ignorance to shocked

understanding. I could have predicted what he would tell me next. But I played out my part.

'What do you mean?'

'The Senora. She had an accent like yours.'

It was a ritual now, a performance.

'Oh, really? What was her name? Do you remember it?'

'It wasn't Spanish. Delio used to call her "Esther." She told me her last name too. Mac-something or other, I can't remember.'

'Not Mackenzie? Esther Mackenzie?'

'Mackenzie! That was it. Esther Mackenzie. How did you know? Have you heard about her before?'

I had been watching him carefully, looking for the slightest false move. But that rocky face, those blue eyes were so innocent. I had not thought of Pablo as the kind of man who would make up stories. I had him figured as one who only speculated or remembered. So I was feeling a little like a boxer who has walked into the Sunday punch of an opponent with no reputation for having a Sunday punch. The best I could do was to hide from him how dazed I was at hearing that name again. I had no doubt, this time, that the Esther Mackenzie he was talking about was one of the Patagonian family. And, I believed now, so must the Amos Mackenzie and the Rachel Mackenzie I had come across. How incredible it all was. And why was it happening? To have found out, in such peculiar circumstances, about the others. To have found out about her in this place, from this man.

I tried, successfully I think, to keep my mask in place

as he told me about the funeral of Delio, and what Esther Mackenzie did, the next morning when she awoke . . .

10

. . . when she awoke, it was after six in the morning. She thought, the parakeets are making enough of a racket to waken the dead. The dead. And here she was, in bed alone. She remembered yesterday's funeral in the heat: the clusters of distressed faces; the cemetery's sterile, red earth and its crop of gravestones; the coffin's elegance deceiving no one, not the mourners, certainly not the ants, which were already crawling around it, sensing the rotting thing within.

Without opening her eyes, she slid her feet to the floor. She did not want to see the other pillow, nor the toes of the well-worn sandals protruding still from under the bedside chair, nor the other paraphernalia of a man's life. She did not want to see the dresser, with his photo, his thin arm around her. She did not want to remember his name. But her mind screamed: 'Delio! Delio! Delio!'

She began her daily rites: the sacrament of washing her body; the sacrament of inhaling the scent of the soap; the sacrament of towelling off; the sacrament of buttoning her black skirt; the sacrament of slipping her feet into her slippers; the sacrament of combing her long hair and pinning it up; the sacrament of making up her eyes, her lips; the sacrament of examining her face in the mirror; the sacrament of tucking in a last stray hair; the sacrament of assessing Esther, dressed for travelling.

She went downstairs, feeling the cool, smooth wood of the bannister run through her hand. She walked along the cool hallway feeling the smooth tiles under her shoes, coolness to coolness. She put her fingers round the front-door handle, smooth and cool to her touch. She opened the door and stepped out onto the veranda, feeling the warmth already in the morning air, the warmth that always preceded another long, hot day. The world was striped with long shadows. Except for her, in the shade of the veranda, except for all those things in shadow, except for the sun, which casts shadows but has none.

The street was quiet. The fishermen had long ago walked down to the shore, and sailed out into the moving waters for the morning catch. She wished them luck, as always. In a half-hour, the wind would begin stirring. She picked up the thick hemp rope, neatly coiled by the rattan couch on the veranda. She carried the rope down the three wooden steps into the yard, the coarse fibre prickling her soft palm.

The car was parked, in its usual place, its front fender almost touching an old palm tree. The tree, its long fronds brown with age, was taller than the house. It had played the part of the old servant who has learnt to cower before unpredictable masters, the wind and the sun.

'How perfect,' she thought.

Then she laid the rope on the ground beside the car, and opened the driver's door, releasing the smell of old leather and motor-oil, and she slid onto the seat, cool against her thighs this early. The keys, already in the ignition, swung slightly from the weight of her body. She made sure the automatic gear was in place before turning the key. The engine growled, then barked, a caged dog excited at the prospect of an unexpected run.

She waited till it was idling smoothly before stepping down onto the driveway again. She dragged one end of the hemp rope towards the old tree. She wound it round and round the comfortable trunk, three times, then knotted it tightly. She took the other end back to the car and fed it through the small steel-framed triangular window in the driver's door. Then she slid into the driver's seat again and slammed the door shut. She pulled most of the slack rope into the car. Through the metal eyelet at the end of the rope, she made a loop big enough for a head.

She sat back and breathed for a moment. Then she lifted the noose and slipped it over her head, being careful not to disturb her hair or the collar of her blouse. She breathed again, deeply, put both hands on the steering wheel, and concentrated on her journey. She felt nothing now, no fear, only emptiness. She was thankful for the gift of emptiness. She revved the engine a few times, rhythmically, to be certain it would not stall.

She was ready.

She watched, for the last time, her right hand, as though it were someone else's. The strong brown fingers gripped the gear knob and shifted it into reverse. The sun was filtering through the palm fronds, and the car hood was flickering like fire. One last, easy breath. Then her foot lifted from the brake and stamped the accelerator to the floor. The car lurched backwards, and by the time it crashed to a halt against the white plaster wall of a house across the street, the thick hemp rope was slack again: but in the course of that brief journey, it had bent the old palm tree more than any hurricane had ever done, before pulling her head right through that little triangular window, ripping it from her body. So that when the neighbours came staggering out to see what had caused the almighty crash, they saw, on the roadway, a length of loose rope attached to a red lump the size of a coconut, trailing a dark mane; and in the car, they saw a stump of body still pumping blood-fountains against the wind-shield that, from where they stood, reflected back the glory of the morning sun.

11

At times, Pablo Renowsky's face had the sculpted appearance of a crude bronze bust. But, as he told me about the death of Esther Mackenzie, his scars did not succeed in undermining his words. He was sniffing more than usual, brushing his broken nose with his thumb, a boxer's habit.

I noticed his blue eyes were moist, and that was unusual for him. He seemed off guard, so I asked him what I had been biding my time to ask.

'Did you ever hear of a scar on the Senora's abdomen?'

His blue eyes cleared instantly, and I saw the surprise in them: now I had revealed a move he had not expected from me.

'A scar? I don't know. Nobody would've known except Delio.'

But he did not pursue me directly, he just circled, waiting to see what else I had to show. And I was watching him, too, but I was also thinking about the curious ways in which I had found out about the fates of each of these Mackenzies, about their deaths: Amos, raving in some bush hospital; Rachel, defying her image in a mirror; and Esther, taking that short, deadly trip.

Pablo began probing, testing me with some rumours he had heard, long ago, about the Senora. Someone, he said, had told him she had been a hooker, at some point. There was another story that she had been a drug-smuggler's woman who shot her man during a quarrel. Pablo had heard these things.

He was watching for my reaction. I confined myself to saying that nothing would surprise me. But the truth was, the inner sponge that absorbs surprises was, in my case, already saturated.

He spoke about the fact that every *agujado* knows he'll some day, almost certainly, die at the hands of his *agujereador*. Yet love between the two was not uncommon. Pablo wondered if that was consoling, to know your lover's hand will also be your killer's.

I looked at him, wondering how serious he was. I tried to read those blue eyes; but now he was the one who was giving nothing away.

12

My last afternoon, before flying north again, I went down to visit Pablo in his hut by the shore. He was lying in his hammock, reading one of his mildewed books. We drank a glass of rum together. I thanked him for all his kindness to me, and especially for telling me about La Cueva and Delio and the Senora. I don't think I would have minded if he had asked me outright the reason for my question about her. But he would never do such a thing. He was much too discreet.

I cannot deny, too, that in spite of my caution (I had given nothing away) and in spite of my confidence that it was only by coincidence that I had found out about these three Mackenzies, yet in a corner of my mind, I was still afraid that Pablo Renowsky, and Doctor Yerdeli, and old JP might be part of some conspiracy that was too frightening to confront sanely.

But all along, Pablo had done the talking. He never once asked about me, about my life. I had presumed at first that this was a defence mechanism learnt in his boxing days. As though we were all opponents in some imaginary ring, where neither sympathy, nor hatred, nor even indifference should be permitted to hamper the outcome.

But, it occurs to me now, he may have been doing just the opposite. Exposing himself completely. Offering me everything he was, so that I would not be afraid to offer a little of myself in return. If that was so, I didn't take the opportunity. Some souls, it seems, will not take chances.

13

But I did open myself to Helen. She and I were ecstatic at being together again. During the weeks we had been apart, she said, she had not exactly enjoyed the sedate menus of family life, the bland stew of unvoiced covenants and assumed hypocrisies. So we threw ourselves together, savouring in each other the sauces we had missed. She stretched towards the warm bowl of southern passion; I, on the other hand, reached for the more northerly dish of endurance and affection. Somewhere half-way through that metaphysical banquet, our appetites sated, we moved on to a shared dessert.

We were lying in bed. It was a cool night, mid-November, and through the big window, we could see that all the stars had been erased by clouds. She had been shocked to hear about Esther. She, too, had no doubt Esther and the other two must have been the Patagonian Mackenzies. We talked about that, for a while, then in general terms about my trip, about Xtepal, about the ancient civilization that had first settled that area, and the retreat of the town to jungle once more. We were having one of our best conversations. Helen was full of her very finest opinions.

'Cultures that are most perfect, are also nearest to disaster. They can't go anywhere but downhill. That's why great nations have the greatest lapses into corruption.'

'Would you apply that to individuals, too?' I asked, for the sake of debate. 'Would you say that a human being who is nearest perfection is on the brink of corruption, too?'

She smiled: 'Of course not. And anyway, the only perfection human beings ever achieve is perfect awareness of their imperfections.'

She was an unpredictable debater.

'You mentioned,' she said, 'that in the old days down there, they used to bury all their buildings every fifty years. I wonder if that should apply to other things. Your Patagonian story, for example. What if it had been better left buried, and not disinterred and dragged into the present?'

165

'Helen, you're full of ideas tonight.'

'Yes. And another thing. As you were telling me Pablo's story, I was thinking, words are the real *agujas*. They penetrate, like skewers, and they can kill.'

We were having fun. But though the earlier metaphysical dinner had satisfied my metaphysical appetite, my body was still hungry.

'Helen,' I said, 'speaking of penetration. Many things penetrate. I have something here, for example, that penetrates. It's a sort of *aguja* too, and you can pierce yourself with it, if you wish.'

I placed her hand on my penis. We then proceded to act out our own private carnival in bed, both taking turns as *agujereadores*, a procedure that seemed, in the end, quite equitable.

Afterwards, I almost mentioned to her that I intended to write to Donald Cromarty again, but I was certain the idea would ruin her sleep. Instead, I proposed that we pay one of our visits to the Paradise Motel. We would travel out to the coast, book in at our usual room, do all the things we loved doing.

Helen said she could think of nothing nicer. A few minutes later she was asleep. I lay there, feeling drowsier and drowsier. I resolved that I would write Donald Cromarty and let him know how I had found out about a certain Esther Mackenzie. I would tell him that both Helen and I were now quite sure that she and the other two Mackenzies I had written him about earlier were the sisters and brother of Zachary Mackenzie. I would ask how his own inquiries were progressing.

I did not realize then, though no one should have understood better, that a letter was no longer necessary. I still did not see what should have been obvious to me, that I was running out of time, and that soon everything would be resolved. Soon, and completely.

Part Five

ZACHARY

Zachary Mackenzie spent several years in 'The Abbey' at the same time as his younger brother, Amos. The elder Mackenzie was shy but fearless. On the night of his thirteenth birthday, for example, on a dare, he climbed a high wall into the village cemetery. Inside, he jumped into a freshly dug grave and retrieved a marked handkerchief left there that afternoon. Another time, he invited a few of the boys to come with him to the orphanage chapel. He hauled himself up onto the altar and, while they watched, undid his fly and urinated over the tabernacle. That act of sacrilege frightened all of the boys.

He came to feel, around the age of fifteen, that the real Zachary Mackenzie was only a shadow of the image he had created of himself. The priests of the Holy Order of Correction were convinced that he was guilty of vanity, for he was often found looking at himself in mirrors. He did not tell them that the configuration of his long, bony nose, the milky blue irises of his narrow eyes, the regular mouth and chin in his slender face gave away nothing, not even to himself.

When it was time to leave the orphanage, he enrolled as an apprentice engineer at a merchant seamen's training school, the SS *Desolation*. In his second year, he was caught naked in bed with the Commodore's motherless daughter, Matilda, sixteen years old. She told her father that in six weeks, the period of her relationship with Zachary Mackenzie, she had learnt more than her father would ever know about what men and women could do to each other. She said that sometimes Zachary could be the most kind and considerate friend she had ever had, and that was what first won her over; sometimes he was an uncontrollable lecher and demanded her body over and over again, till she was too raw to take any more; sometimes he was a stern moralist, preaching at her, repent, repent; sometimes he was a sadist and tied her to the bed, lashed her with his belt, and bit her nipples, and raped her; sometimes he cringed and wept before her, and begged her soak him in her urine and rub her feces in his hair; sometimes he was a stranger and refused to acknowledge her, denying he had ever been intimate with her. They had both been virgins at the beginning of that summer.

Zachary Mackenzie, expelled from SS *Desolation*, found a berth as an engineer with a small shipping line. He was efficient with the crew, but in the officer's mess, his fellow officers did not know what to think of him. His words were often a camouflage he used to obscure his meaning. This opaqueness irritated some but was oddly comforting to others. On voyages, he was an avid reader, a journal-keeper. He met the rest of his family only once, after leaving the orphanage.

Notebook, A. McGAW

1

Around midnight the following night, I was in such a deep sleep that Helen had to wake me to answer the phone in the study next door to our bedroom. I was in the middle of a confusing dream in which I was at a party with some friends, but none of them seemed to know who I was, and when I tried to talk to them, to ask what was the matter, I could not hear my own voice.

I stumbled into the study to answer the phone, still half in that dream. Vaguely I noticed that the night was dark, and it must have been raining, for I could hear the occasional hiss of a passing car on the road outside. I picked up the phone.

'Hello?' What a relief. I could hear myself. The dream was over.

'Ezra, sorry to disturb you. This is Donald Cromarty speaking.'

The soft Highland voice. I should have been surprised, but I was not, so I had to make myself sound surprised.

'Cromarty! How are you?'

For a while, we bartered long-distance courtesies, till he got round to telling me why he had phoned.

'It's about the four Mackenzies.'

As though it could have been about anything else. I waited politely for him to go on.

'I've found a man with information on the eldest one, Zachary. I can't get him to tell me anything, but he's genuine. He knew the names of all four. He said Isabel Jaggard told him to get in touch with me. You won't know her, but she was prominent here at one time. That's all he'd tell me. He said he'd talk to both of us together, or not at all. So it's up to you. Can you get away?'

2

The plane circled over the airport at nine in the morning. We had been travelling for hours, at thirty thousand feet, through an endless desert of detergent suds. But as the plane descended, it was suddenly at the underbelly of a dark monster that suckled, from its gloomy udders, the blunt, green hills of the land below. We landed unobtrusively and skulked along the runway to our refuge near the comforting lights of the terminal.

Enter, at last, Donald Cromarty!

He was waiting at Arrivals. He was an easy man to spot. Tall, stooped, his face a pitted battlefield from a childhood war with smallpox. His hair, I noticed, now lay in wisps across his head, and that suited him. His whole body, in fact, had at last caught up with a mind that had matured long before. The cautious smile, the soft voice remained the same. I told him it was good to see him after all these years. We greeted each other, and, if I had not noticed a hardness in his green eyes that was new to me, I might actually have felt comforted, I might even have felt at home.

3

We drove east towards the capital in his old Mercedes, passing through the dirty towns of the industrial waste-land. The highway was excellent, an expensive chain looping together a score of coal-cinders. We talked, and the journey passed quickly.

Cromarty told me how he had set out, so many months ago, to make inquiries about the Mackenzies. I had guessed right about the dead ends he had run into: archives incinerated in wartime bombing raids; the depopulation of the western islands, so that witnesses were impossible to find; the problem of pinpointing which one of several islands suited the needs of my grandfather Daniel Stevenson's story.

But what most frustrated Cromarty was the lack of

any written reference to the alleged crime. He found it hard to accept that the press had ever been *that* discreet. He had checked out Mackenzies of every sort. He had speculated, on the basis of what I'd told him, that Zachary, with his notebooks and his liking for story-telling, might even have turned in the end to writing as a career. Cromarty had inquired into the lives of at least five hundred writing Mackenzies, in vain.

The break came when he decided to use, for his own ends, the very medium that had thwarted him. He placed a notice in *The Northern News*. His message was clear enough: he wanted to find out about a domestic crime somewhere in the islands about the turn of the century; the name of the family involved was Mackenzie; the father was a doctor, and the four children were called Amos, Rachel, Esther, and Zachary.

The next day, a man telephoned and asked exactly why Cromarty was interested. Cromarty told him about me. The man said his friend Isabel Jaggard had encour-aged him to help, but that he was afraid of legal liability, so he needed absolute confidentiality. Cromarty knew who Isabel Jaggard was, gave the assurances, and arranged the meeting to which we were now on our way.

I, in turn, told Cromarty about my trip south, my discovery of Esther Mackenzie, and my certainty that she and Amos and Rachel were the Patagonian Mackenzies.

Cromarty shook his head when I had finished. He'd never come across such a set of events, he said, with so many strange interlinkings and coincidences.

Cromarty was certainly not the type to balk at the strange. He was the historian who had found proof of the existence, several centuries ago, of a group of hitherto unknown hermit monks who had lived out their perverse sanctity (they mutilated their bodies as part of their spiritual journey) on the islands off the west coast. That piece of scholarly detective work had gained him international prestige.

So when he said he was troubled, I felt uncomfortable, as though I needed to justify myself. I kept quiet, but I was afraid he doubted the truth of what I'd told him, from the start. It ran through my head that perhaps he didn't even believe I'd heard the story from Daniel Stevenson. I hoped that now he had uncovered someone else who knew about Zachary Mackenzie, he might be convinced I had not been making things up.

As though he could read my mind, Cromarty insisted that he intended to unravel the Mackenzie mystery, 'no matter where it may lead.' He said this several times, glancing at me. I kept my misgivings, and my reasons for them, to myself.

After about an hour, we arrived earlier than we had expected, in the capital. I booked into a small hotel off Duchess Street, and told him I'd like to stretch out for a few hours. I was tired after the rigours of a sleepless night-flight. Cromarty said he would be happy to pass away the hours before our meeting browsing in the various bookstores around the city.

4

I rested well, and, round six o'clock, Cromarty and I hurried down to the meeting place, a bar just a few blocks away. We hurried, for it was the middle of November, pitch dark, and a chill wind from the nearby Firth was funnelling its familiar, squally rain, into the city. Austerity in all things, it howled.

We were happy to get inside the doors of The Last Minstrel. Through a haze of cigarette and pipe smoke, I looked around. It was a respectable bar, one wall bristling with dusty claymores and targes on a tartan cloth whose veins seemed to have been bled, long ago, by a handful of rusty skean-dhus. On another wall, a dozen brown portraits looked out at us. They might have been the ancestors of the handful of gloomy customers (none of them women) who sat at plastic tables along the walls.

But the place was warm, at least. Cromarty and I went to one of the corner tables and began to thaw our chilled bones with lukewarm whisky. We had just settled down, when the door opened, allowing the cold air a vindictive foray. The cause of the draught was the entry of a very elderly man and woman. He was wearing a tweed coat, and the woman was dressed in black. She was white haired and white faced, and wore sun-glasses. The man was reddish and stocky for his age. He looked around, saw us looking at him, and, taking a firm grip on the old woman's elbow, as though he had done it often before, led her towards our table.

'Professor?' he said.

Cromarty rose, and the man spoke again, in a throaty voice.

'My name is Gib Douglas, I talked to you on the phone. This is Isabel Jaggard.'

Cromarty introduced me. The old woman, Isabel Jaggard, said nothing, did not extend her hand to us, nor did she see our hands. She was blind. Gib Douglas helped her into a chair, in that familiar way, and we all sat down. Cromarty and I felt a little awkward at her silence. But she continued to say nothing. She just sat, gathering herself, slightly out of breath. Her white face was pinched from the cold night air. I couldn't help noticing her lips, how red they were, red as a healthy child's, at odds with the rest of her old woman's face. The rain had pimpled her dark glasses: naturally, she did not wipe them.

Gib Douglas went to the bar for drinks, then sat beside me. He looked like a man of action gone to seed, yet somehow too jumpy for an ex-soldier or an ex-policeman. He was clearly not happy about being with us. He drank a whisky down with hands that had a molten appearance to them. They guided Isabel Jaggard's hand to the glass of port she had asked for, and she picked it up and sipped at it slowly. He lit a cigarette for himself as she began to talk in a deep contralto voice, with only a slight tremor of age in it.

She wanted to ask me some questions. Who was I exactly? Why did I have such an interest in the Mackenzie family? What would I do with the information if I got it?

179

What did I already know about Zachary Mackenzie? Or think I knew?

This brief litany of questions flowed from a mouth that did not match the wilting face. I was so entranced by her mouth that I hardly noticed when it was no longer moving. Till she took off her dark glasses and laid them clumsily on the table. Her eyes were white, bulging, the dead irises staring outwards towards her left and right sides, like a rabbit's eyes.

I briefly told her everything I thought she should know, about how as a boy I had heard the story of the Mackenzies first from my grandfather, Daniel Stevenson; and how, as I grew up, I came to presume it was nothing but a story. Till I met Doctor Yerdeli at the Institute for the Lost, and she mentioned the name Amos Mackenzie, and told me about his fate. And that made me wonder, and I decided to enlist the help of Cromarty.

Cromarty had heard all this before, but he was listening and was watching me just the same. Gib Douglas just went on looking nervous, drinking and smoking, building himself up for something unpleasant. I do not know what Isabel Jaggard thought of my story. Her white face and blind eyes no longer served as a means of expression. But her head was cocked to one side while I talked, which I guessed was a sign she was interested.

I told her about my more recent discoveries of two other Mackenzies, Rachel and Esther, who certainly had the right names and might be from the same family. And I told her how they died. Once or twice, when I paused, she would shake her head.

'Is that so? Is that so?'

When I had said everything I had to say, Isabel Jaggard pursed those lips that looked sometimes to me like twin bloodsuckers wriggling in the middle of a dead face. She spoke again.

'Professor Cromarty's work is well known. Even though I can't read any more, I am read to, daily. Isn't that so, Gib?'

The question slid sensually through her lips.

'When I heard,' she said, 'that the professor was making inquiries about the Mackenzie family, I thought maybe it was time to clear the air, before all those who knew were dead.'

So she advised Gib Douglas to respond to the advertisement, and found out that I was at the root of it. She aimed the words in my direction:

'I knew you had to be here when the truth was told,' she said. I felt uncomfortable, for Cromarty was watching me. But she continued:

'I've never talked about any of this before, except to Gib. I persuaded him it wouldn't be a bad thing to put the facts in the hands of people who wouldn't exploit them for the wrong reasons.'

I had no idea what the wrong reasons might be, or the right ones, for that matter. But I asked her, please, to proceed.

'Years ago,' she said, 'I was a publisher in this city. During the lifetime when I could still see.'

That blank face was incapable of showing bitterness.

'I still think of myself as looking the way I looked

181

then. My hair was brown, and my eyes were green. Gib occasionally tells me how I look now, don't you Gib? That's one advantage of blindness. You can't see yourself getting old. You can't see somebody else's disgust.'

Her lips were juicily red as she said that. Gib Douglas glanced at her, but I could not tell what he was thinking.

'Someone in my family has been in the publishing business somewhere since the sixteenth century. I tried to keep the tradition going. I inherited some money, and started a small publishing house here. I knew it would never make me rich. Money down the drain, that's what they said. It's true, any publisher will tell you that.'

I noticed her voice was a little less deep, a little lighter when she spoke about those early days, about the time when she wasn't long out of university and was trying to get the business started, hunting everywhere for good manuscripts to publish. She remembered the morning a man came through her office door on High Street. He was a tall, thin-faced man of about fifty, and he had a brown envelope with him, containing his manuscript. He told her he'd been writing on and off for twenty years, ever since he retired from the sea, that he'd been a ship's engineer for years. He'd had no luck having anything published.

He said his name was Zachary Mackenzie.

'I told him I was willing to take a look at his manuscript, but I wouldn't make any promises. I said I'd be in touch with him. And he left.'

Cromarty and I sat in that cheerless bar and waited while the hands of Gib Douglas closed Isabel Jaggard's fingers, caressingly, round her glass of port. Cromarty watched silently, and I wondered what he was thinking. Here was solid, eye-witness (she could see then) proof that at least one Mackenzie, Zachary, had existed. Perhaps still did. Cromarty did not look at me.

Isabel Jaggard was in no rush. She was composing the order of events, this being her first telling of the story. Her rabbit eyes seemed to assess her flanks and find nothing to worry about. She breathed deeply and went on to tell us how she took Zachary Mackenzie's manuscript home with her that night and read it over.

5

She saw immediately it was no best-seller. The novel, entitled *The Cells*, was a brief, turgid account of life in a penal colony. The language was archaic and the characters quite unbelievable: a man, for instance, who had planted a forest of artificial trees; a witch who had vomited up all kinds of things, including books and pistols; a mayoress who had encouraged her citizens to exchange their identities with each other, whenever they felt the need, till they forgot who they originally were; a prison warden who was no less eccentric than the prisoners.

Even if the novel had some merit, Isabel Jaggard was

well aware that the times were not right for it. The Great Depression was not long past. But more important, the nationalist movement was in full swing. People were in the mood for books that encouraged optimism and patriotism, not for obscure fantasies such as *The Cells*.

Yet there was something Isabel Jaggard liked about the book, she was not sure why. So, even though her fledgling business sense winced at her recklessness, something she liked to think of as the mature, aesthetic part of her goaded her on to publish it.

Even in those early days, she always made a principle of getting to know her authors intimately. Accordingly, she met Zachary Mackenzie several times on the understanding that the manuscript was not to be mentioned. It was only after a while, when she knew him better and was satisfied with his potential, that she arranged to meet him at her office and told him her official decision to publish his novel. The man was elated. She tried to warn him against great expectations. She said:

'Zachary, in all honesty, this is hardly a novel. It's really just a group of short stories loosely tied together.'

She was surprised at how quick he was to defend himself. He said: 'That's what life is, anyway: a handful of short stories pretending to be a novel.'

When she asked him for a few more facts about his background for publicity, he became very reluctant to talk. In spite of how often she had met him, how well she knew him, he had not been willing to tell much about his earlier life. All she was able to get out of him was that there had been a tragedy in his family, and that he and his sisters and brother were sent to orphanages, and that he had ended up as an engineer on various merchant ships.

Then he had looked at her with his milky blue eyes and made a special plea. He had said he would take it as a great favour if she would abstain from using any of the vague information he had given her. Because he did not want his book published under his own name. His own name was one he preferred to forget. He would like to use the pseudonym, 'Archie McGaw'.

At the time, Isabel Jaggard was surprised, and thought the name a little peculiar. But she could see no real objection, so long as he would continue to publish under the name of Archie McGaw. He promised he would.

In the next few years she published three of his novels, *The Cells, Captain Jack*, and *The Feast*, none of them very successful. But the nationalists had taken notice of Archie McGaw. They picked on him, time and time again, denouncing his books for being irrelevant, and gloomy.

Isabel Jaggard advised him to do what others in his shoes had done, and pay no attention. She told him these kinds of political movements depended upon order and conformity. That they were the antithesis of life and art. But he wouldn't keep quiet. That stubbornness was a side of him she had noticed whenever she tried to make editorial changes to his books. So, with the nationalists, he did the worst possible thing. He wrote letters to all the newspapers and to the major literary magazine, *The Homeland*, pleading for tolerance and fairness. That just seemed to stir up even more hostility towards him. The editor of *The Homeland*, a man named Angus Cameron, never missed a chance after that to make unkind remarks about Archie McGaw.

But a most extraordinary thing happened. His most recent novel, *The Feast*, and then his previous two started to sell, really sell. Isabel Jaggard couldn't keep up with the demand. Every bookstore in the area was requesting fresh supplies, daily, of anything by Archie McGaw. His books had been gathering dust in her warehouse, so she was delighted to see them go. By the end of one single week, they were all gone, and she began making plans for second printings. It looked as though the career of Archie McGaw was at last taking off.

6

Now Isabel Jaggard turned to Gib Douglas, who was sitting there, looking more nervous than ever, in spite of all the whisky. Her deep voice took on a wheedling tone. She told him she knew it was hard for him, but he should tell his story now and get it over with. He went to get himself another drink first.

Donald Cromarty at last spoke. 'Now I know why I couldn't find a reference to any Zachary Mackenzie in the library holdings. I should have thought of the possibility of a pseudonym.'

I myself took advantage of the delay to ask her some questions.

'Did Zachary ever mention his trip to Patagonia?'

'I don't remember, he may have. He had been in so many places.'

'Did he ever say anything explicitly about his family or the murder of his mother?'

'No.'

Gib Douglas came back to the table with his drink.

'Maybe we should let Gib tell what he knows,' Isabel Jaggard said. 'And while he's talking, I'll try and think of anything else that might be of interest to you.'

Gib Douglas rumbled, drank the whisky down, and inhaled deeply from his cigarette. He looked at Isabel Jaggard, then at the backs of his hands, and he was ready. He began to speak in his throaty voice.

7

'I was a student, back then, and I joined the nationalists. We talked a lot, that was all, and painted slogans on the walls of the railway stations. But it was more exciting than sitting at lectures.'

Gib Douglas laughed the nervous laugh of a man who's on his way to telling something that won't be very funny. His hand, the one holding the cigarette, was trembling, and he noticed and wished that it wouldn't. Isabel Jaggard was listening to him with her head tilted. Her red lips were slightly apart.

'We were told to kidnap Archie McGaw (that was the only name I knew him by). As a kind of practical joke. I'd never even read any of his books. Angus Cameron was in charge of our group, and he hated McGaw's guts. That was good enough for us. I volunteered to help with the kidnapping, for the fun of it.

'We drove over to McGaw's place around midnight on a July night. He lived up one of the closes in the Old Town. There was nobody around at that time of night, but we were scared.'

The telling of his story changed Gib Douglas. He himself was only a word in it, but he wanted the story to be a good setting for that word. He had been nervous and uncertain a few minutes ago. Now he was engrossed in his narrative, manipulating it, trying to make it effective and memorable, glancing at Isabel Jaggard, his real audience, anxious to satisfy her.

'We sneaked up the close stairs and pried open McGaw's door. It was only a one-room flat, and he was lying there on the bed. We just went over and grabbed him. I saw right away he was wide awake, but he didn't try to get away or shout for help. He just lay there, terrified, looking up at us. He was alone in bed . . .'

8

... he was alone in bed, as he had been for years now. He was afraid, but not very much, when the two men wearing wool masks bent over him. But he thought it would be wiser to look terrified, so he did. He could tell from their movements they were young. He would have liked to put his housecoat on over his pyjamas when he realized they were going to take him away, but they tied his hands behind him with a piece of electrical wire. He would have liked to ask them why they wanted him. But the square of sticking plaster they had stretched over his mouth stopped his lips from moving and made his words a groan.

One of the masks, a stockily built young man, spoke in a throaty whisper.

'Shut up! Or I'll shut you up.'

They shuffled him downstairs, his legs not quite awake yet, his bare feet tender on the cold paving, and pushed him into the back of a car. It was an old, black car with torn leather seats. It lurched forward and began to chew up, with uneven gulps, the deserted cobble-stone streets of the city, then it drank down smoothly the black-tops of the country roads to the south.

He was only a little afraid, so he was able to consider everything quite calmly. He knew they must be nationalists. Did they really think anyone would pay money for his release? He couldn't believe they were that misguided. Perhaps the recent, unexpected popularity of his books had made him worth kidnapping, for some symbolic reason. Because he was only slightly afraid, he allowed himself to think: what an irony, what an unintended compliment, if, after all the abuse they'd lumped on him, he was now successful enough for them to want to kidnap him!

About twenty miles south of the city, whenever the moon broke through the high clouds, he could make out, through the car window, stunted hills that protruded from the landscape like the burial mounds of mountains. They were the kinds of hills he liked to set his novels among. This was the country, and because he was only a little afraid, he felt more and more at home. The car slowed, swerved onto a dirt road that wasn't much more than a scar on a hillside, and jolted along for a mile or two. It stopped beside a fieldstone dike with an opening in it. Silence.

The shapes of a dozen other parked cars lurked nearby. The stockier of his two kidnappers opened the back door.

'Get out!'

He stumbled out, feeling his age, his bare feet revolting at every prickle and stone. The man prodded him through the opening in the dike, along a winding sheep-path in a field, and up a rise. The air was clear and fresh. He could smell heather and smoke. The moorlands for miles around were playing hide-and-seek with the moon.

For the first time since the two men entered his apartment an hour ago, the thought crossed his mind that perhaps something very unpleasant was going to happen to him. Not that he was any more afraid. Just curious.

As he would have been about one of his stories when he had just begun writing it and had no idea what would happen next.

He could see down in the valley, about a hundred yards away, a blazing bonfire and several dozen people milling about. The stocky man began shouting to them, straining his throat.

'Hey! We've got him! We've got him.'

The distant faces, dark faces turned towards them descending.

The two men jostled him down to where the group stood silent and still, watching. The fire, like a beacon misplaced in a valley, was huge, the logs on it crackling loudly, the only noise in that cool night. The group were all wearing woollen masks and sometimes the whites of their eyes would catch the fire-light. The stocky man gave him a last push, causing him to sprawl over a mound just a few yards from the fire.

He caught a glimpse of the mound as he fell, just before the acute corners and the ruler-sharp edges confirmed, on his flesh, what he had glimpsed. It was a mound of books. The flat surfaces of some of them supported him comfortingly for a moment, but others made him slide, the harder he tried to stand up to balance himself, his hands still tied behind his back. Then the entire hillock of books opened and half-swallowed him.

His bare toes touched the ground. He got up on his knees and slithered out of the mound, like a creature it had given birth to. On his feet now, he recognized, whenever the flickering light would allow his eyes to focus, that some of the books were his own. He could make out the spines of his latest, *The Feast*. He could see some copies of *Captain Jack* and *The Cells*.

Truth crept up on him in a gentle way at first. Before gathering speed and slamming right into him, making him sob. *All* of the books in that mound were his: *he Fe, ast, in Ja, ell, The C, tain, ack, ie Mc, s Arc, ells Ar, ck Arc, east Ar, Gaw, ack, McGa, ack, ack.* Bits and pieces of his name, his titles, inverted or at awkward angles, but all his. He was full of dread. Where had they all come from, so many? Sick at heart, he understood.

'Yes, they're all yours,' said a voice louder than the crackling fire, from the other side of the mound. In spite of the mask, he knew the thin voice of Angus Cameron, the editor of *The Homeland*.

'We bought up every copy. We ordered them from every bookstore in the city. It took us a couple of weeks to get them all. How does it feel to be so popular?'

In the fire's heat, he shivered and looked across the heap of his collected works, not a very large heap. He did not want to hear any more. But Cameron came round to his side of the mound. Through the holes in the mask, he could see those familiar, contemptuous eyes.

'Surely you didn't think anybody in their right mind would want to read this trash? Especially the last one.'

He prodded a copy of *The Feast* with his boot, the way a man prods something repulsive, a turd.

'This one was even worse than the others. We had to spend a lot of money buying them all up, but it was worth it, to save anybody else from having to read them.'

The other masks were laughing at him, taunting. He had nothing to say, absolutely nothing. But he heard a noise coming from his sealed mouth, in spite of himself, the sound of all of his words, trapped together, making a single moan.

'We thought you'd like to see how much we value your books,' said Cameron.

He signalled to the others (some of whom, from their clothes, their voices, were women). They began picking up armfuls of books from the mound and tossing them into the bonfire.

He watched all this, as though in a dream the books flapping their covers uselessly like crippled birds, exploding in the fire, sending up flares into the night air, in vain, for there was no one to rescue them. He watched the burning of his books, just tarted-up firewood, after all. The waves of heat billowed towards him, the acrid smoke blew back in his face, stinging his eyes and nose. The fire crackled and the stokers laboured. Till all the fuel was gone, and they stood enjoying the blaze.

As he ran forward, he saw for a moment another fire long ago, amongst hills just like these, a ring of men gathered around it, all dead men now, nothing of them remaining any more. He ran and jumped with all his strength into the heat and the noise, pumping his knees, running up the hill of fire, feeling nothing, till suddenly the flames were scalpels slicing at his white bare feet, and his legs, and his white belly, and his face, and most horrifying of all, his hands still tied behind him. But he did not scream as his own words devoured him cannibalizing their maker, devouring themselves too, though some of them rose again, not phoenixes, just wisps of ashy paper, floating off, disintegrating in the darkness, and in the night air.

9

Gib Douglas rested his head in his molten hands for a moment, and breathed deeply. But he was not finished.

Archie McGaw, he said, jumping into the fire, carried with him the youth of most of those who watched him. They stood paralysed. Gib Douglas and his partner tried to go in after McGaw, but those thousands of books burnt so fiercely, they could not penetrate the borders of the fire. So they raked at the blaze with long pieces of lumber, hoping somehow to snare his body. But it was no use. They could only watch him in there among his books, burning. Above the crackle of the fire, they could hear his body sizzling, they could see the flames shoot upwards, feasting on his melting flesh. Gib Douglas, in desperation, reached in and gripped one of the legs, but to the horror of everyone, the foot tore off at the ankle when he pulled.

By the time they did get Archie McGaw out, he was nothing but a charred carcass, with the ends of some bones protruding. They left him out there on the moors, beside the remains of the fire, and drove home, silent (Angus Cameron had not said a word since McGaw jumped into the fire). A few days later, a shepherd saw his collie sniffing at the blackened lump beside the ashes, and called the police.

The body was never identified. The investigation was not very thorough, perhaps because the police quickly found out that the sons and daughters of some very influential people were involved. In the end, the coroner said that the death was most likely a suicide, though the fire seemed extravagant, and there were signs a number of people had stood by. The newspapers said little about the affair, for that was a time when much more momentous events were happening throughout Europe. So Archie McGaw's death passed unnoticed as his literary career.

But, Gib Douglas said, nothing was ever the same after that. He and some of his friends were finished with the nationalists, or any other party for that matter. He spent a week in hospital with badly burnt hands. But even thirty years had not healed the real wound. Angus Cameron, in time, recovered his nerve and tried to coax Gib and the others to rejoin the movement.

A tender heart, he said, is a luxury no true patriot can afford.

10

Gib Douglas was done with his story. He had never before told anyone except Isabel Jaggard what he knew about the death of Archie McGaw. He had tried for years not even to think about it. He drank down another quick whisky. He looked towards Isabel Jaggard. Could they go now?

No. First, she wanted us to know that it wasn't till a month after the burning, when she tried to get in touch with Zachary Mackenzie, that she realized he was missing. It had crossed her mind the burnt body on the moors might be his, but she kept her suspicions to herself.

'Everybody knew the nationalists had something to do with it. So I let it go. At that time, you didn't know who you could trust. I never heard the truth till Gib told me. By then, who cared about Zachary Mackenzie or Angus Cameron or the body on the moors?'

I wanted Gib Douglas to tell me something.

'Do you know whether he had a scar on his abdomen?'

He looked at me for a moment, then turned his eyes

towards Isabel Jaggard. She could not see what we could see, the bitterness in his face.

'I'm not the one you should ask,' he said.

Isabel Jaggard's impenetrable eyes rolled. Gib Douglas stood up, buttoned his coat, and moved round to help her out of her chair.

But when she felt his hand on her arm, she told him to wait a minute. She said something had just come back to her. She had thought of it earlier, when I told them my grandfather Daniel Stevenson's story. And just now, when I asked Gib Douglas about the scar, she thought of it again. On the day she told Zachary Mackenzie she wanted to publish his first book, when he asked if he could use the name Archie McGaw instead, she had asked him why he didn't want to use his own name. He said, as far as he was concerned, his real name, Zachary Mackenzie, would be like a scar on the belly of his book.

'That was exactly what he said: "a scar on its belly." ' Her eyes were bulging more than usual and her lips were wet with the phrase.

'At the time, I said to him, what a strange notion. He said it might seem strange to me, but there were other people who wouldn't think it was so strange.' Gib Douglas helped her to her feet, and they moved towards the door. As they were leaving The Last Minstrel, just an old couple again, she called out that I should visit her next morning, and she would pass on to me whatever relics of Zachary Mackenzie were left in her files. She was certain she had at least a photograph.

197

11

Gib Douglas pushed the door open, letting them out and a scouring draught in. The brown portraits looked down their disapproval of Cromarty and me for staying on for a last drink. Cromarty had been so quiet, I felt I must talk.

'What a horrible fate,' I said.

'Whose?' he asked. Taking me by surprise.

'Well, Zachary Mackenzie's.'

'Quite.'

He was silent. So for want of anything better to say, I asked: 'Do you think Isabel Jaggard and Zachary Mackenzie were lovers? The way Gib Douglas looked at her, when I asked about the scar.'

Cromarty, half-quizzical, inspected my face.

'What difference does it make?'

I was going to ask what exactly he meant by that. In fact, I was going to ask him what was going on in his head, his whole attitude was so strange. And perhaps I would have. But he had made up his mind now to talk, or at least to ask some questions, and he began asking them.

'Let me get this straight. You say that Zachary Mackenzie met your grandfather, Daniel Stevenson, years ago in Patagonia?'

'Yes.'

'And he told your grandfather the story of a murder and its effects on four children, one of them being himself?'

'Yes.'

198

'And your grandfather, in turn, told the story to you?'

I agreed.

'And it looks now as though all four Mackenzie children died violent or abnormal deaths?'

'Yes, I suppose it does.'

'And you found out about all of these deaths in the course of just the past few months?'

Again, I agreed.

He stopped, as if running my answers over in his head. His eyes, I felt, were not friendly, and I was nervous under their scrutiny. He said:

'I'm sure you would agree with me that certain things are puzzling. Principally the fact that in spite of all we've found out about the four children, it hasn't been possible to find any evidence whatever of the original crime?'

I agreed. What else could I do?

'Finally, you would concur that in the case of all four children, no one has been able to attest to the presence of scars on their abdomens?'

I could hardly disagree with that. In fact, I might have asked him, haven't I been the one who put the question in all four cases? But I was busy steeling myself for his next logical question.

To my relief, he did not ask it. The interrogation was over.

Still, I had not much liked being subjected to his cross-examination, so I asked him if he was implying something by it.

'No, I am implying nothing,' he said. His voice was calm, and he was choosing his words carefully. He said there was really no need to imply anything any more. The truth was almost apparent to him, and would be to me, too, if I were to examine the facts carefully.

'The truth will out,' he said.

I told him, without hesitation, that I had no idea what he meant. He said that was a pity, and he stood up. It was time for him to go, for he had to drive back west.

We went outside into the rain, but that was better than sitting under those scowling portraits on the wall of The Last Minstrel. We walked in the downpour to where his old Mercedes was parked, in a lane near my hotel.

We shook hands. He said he'd enjoyed my visit and the meeting with Isabel Jaggard and Gib Douglas. I tried my best to read his face in the street lights. But the rain was filling in his pock-marks, giving him the smooth face of a stranger. I promised I'd write him when I got back home, if I found anything of interest in Isabel Jaggard's files. As he slid into the car, he said one last thing.

'I think everything will be settled quite soon.'

His familiar face, now that he was out of the rain, had reappeared. He smiled, and nodded, pulled the car door shut, and drove away. As his car receded along the street, my peace of mind returned from its hiding place.

Part Six

THE PARADISE
MOTEL

1

The next morning, I got up early, breakfasted, then walked
under a low, grey sky to Isabel Jaggard's house, one of
those respectable old terrace houses with exteriors modest
enough not to stir up too much envy. Gib Douglas opened
the door. He had the sour look of a man with a hangover
confronting the dog that bit him. He led me into a sombre,
mahogany-panelled parlour where Isabel Jaggard, in her
dark glasses, was sitting on a couch in front of a fire. The
yellow brocade curtains were drawn back, and so was the
neck of her housecoat, enough to give a glimpse of a thin
pair of breasts. She patted the couch for me to sit beside
her. I noticed, as I sat down, a faint odour, neither pleasant
nor unpleasant, coming from her.

She said Gib had searched around amongst the boxes
in the attic and had found, as she knew he would, the
old Archie McGaw file. The cardboard file-folder lay on
a small rectangular table beside the couch. I had noticed
the table when I came in, because its shape and the
brass handles that adorned it gave it the appearance
of a child's coffin. She told me to take a look inside
the folder, and I did. It contained two large, unsealed
manila envelopes. I opened the thinner of the two,
and slid out an enlarged photograph, a little brown
on the edges (it must have been half a century old)
but very professional looking.

'Is that the picture?' she asked.

'Yes.'

2

Two young men flank two young women standing on a Persian rug in front of a blank white wall. The wall might be in a studio, or a restaurant, or a theatre. On the left of the picture, the one who seems slightly the elder of the two men stands wearing a high-collared uniform. He is tall and thin-faced, with a drooping moustache. His eyelids are narrow, his eyes barely visible. His bent right arm ends abruptly at a white shirt-cuff by the jacket pocket. On the other side of the picture, the younger man stands. He is wearing a dress-suit, a bow tie, and spats. He too is thin-faced, but with large, sad eyes and unruly hair. His left hand rests on the stem of a rubber-plant beside him. In spite of their formal pose, the two men are deliberately not looking at the camera. Next to the younger man, not touching him (there is a space between each of the four), stands the younger woman. She is fair-haired and slight. She wears a long coat with a fur trim at the collar. She is watching, fascinated, something not in the picture. The other woman, beside her, is the only one watching the camera. She is solidly built, with a square face and dark hair. She wears a dark suit, and a fur stole fastened by a long, ornamental pin. The four might be friends posing successfully as strangers, or strangers posing unsuccessfully as friends.

3

Isabel Jaggard groped for my leg, bending far enough in my direction to reveal those thin breasts even more. The smell she gave off was slightly musky. She hoped the photograph was helpful, and was so sorry she couldn't give me copies of Mackenzie's novels. Gib Douglas had not been able to find any, though she was sure she had them in a box somewhere. She cocked her head, and I saw him enter the room from another door. He did not say anything, but came over and stood by the fire, examining his hands. Isabel Jaggard, kneading my thigh, said that if I looked hard enough, one or two of the novels might still be found in used-book stores.

The other envelope, she said, contained a manuscript Zachary Mackenzie had given her just a week before his disappearance. I was welcome to it. It wasn't a completed work, just some journal notes Zachary Mackenzie said he'd made when he was at sea.

I accepted the two envelopes with thanks. She was feeling around for my hand, so I clasped hers. How warm it was, how moist, despite the wrinkled skin. Her lips were red and wet. Because of the way she had twisted herself, her robe had opened at her thighs, and I could see wiry legs and a wisp of steel-grey pubic hair. The dark plastic of her glasses threw back twin distorted reflections of myself. They also reflected two Gib Douglases watching. I quickly withdrew my hand from hers, stood up, said goodbye, and went to the door. I noticed, in the hallway, a large framed black and white photograph of a striking woman with fine features, noticeable eyes, and slightly pouted lips. Of course. Isabel Jaggard, as she must once have looked.

When that heavy wooden door closed softly behind me, I stopped on the top step to turn up my collar, for it was very cold, as though there might even be snow. That was when, I could swear, I heard singing coming from inside the house. I may have been wrong, for a car was going past at that moment. But if Gib Douglas and Isabel Jaggard were capable of singing, I think that is how they would have sounded: a contralto and a throaty bass in a sinister duet. I strained my ears to hear the sound again. Nothing. I took a deep breath of the cold air, then with the envelopes under my arm, I started down the tunnel of grey light that was the street.

4

It never did snow that day. I spent much of the time walking, shopping for a gift for Helen (I found one in a little antique shop, a sixteenth-century anthology of poems, entitled, simply, *Poemes*, with an inscription in fading ink on the inside cover: 'I am not I: pity the tale of me'). I climbed the hill to the squat castle and looked out from the ramparts down at the huddled city. The clouds, the trees, the chimney smoke made visible the stinging wind from the Firth.

I must have walked for hours that afternoon. By eight o'clock, I was feeling hungry, for I had not eaten since breakfast. I found a pub, a cheerful-looking one (no sad portraits on the walls), and ate a pub dinner: a pint of beer, a meat pie brimming with peas, and chips. I felt good.

But by the time I got back to the hotel, around ten o'clock, my stomach was a little queasy. Perhaps jet-lag was the cause, or walking too long on an empty stomach, or eating too quickly. I went to bed right away, and tried to force myself to sleep. But the longer I lay there, the worse I felt: a pain was developing that made me feel too sick even to take a sip of water.

Around two in the morning, the pain was very bad. I probed around my stomach lightly with my fingertips in the area of the appendix. Nothing. But, just below the navel, my fingers brushed against something. I switched on the lamp. Yes, there it was. A protrusion, an angular sort of protrusion right in the middle of my belly, a place where no angles should exist, straining against the flesh. My god. I tried not to panic. But as I looked, I could swear I saw the thing move.

Sick with fear, I phoned the front desk and told the receptionist I needed help.

By the time the hotel porter admitted two ambulance attendants into my room, I had already vomited a mixture of meat pie and blood onto the linoleum floor. The ambulance men loaded me, slightly feverish but still aware of everything, onto a stretcher and wheeled me along the spongy carpeted corridor into the elevator with its aura of dead cigarettes; then through the door of the hotel, into the chill.

The ride in the ambulance must have been only a few minutes, but it was an eternity of pain and fear. I was certain I could feel the thing moving around in my belly, making itself intimate with the raw inside of my body.

As they lifted me out of the ambulance and wheeled me into Emergency, each jolt forced a scream out of me. My belly was about to explode. I could see a haze of white and green shapes, I could feel fingers touching me, I could hear soothing voices and questions I could not answer, for fear my words would turn into vomit. Once or twice, I heard a deep male voice.

'We'll need consent.'

And the same voice again, later, deeper still.

'If we don't go ahead, he'll die on us.'

Then I was gliding along endless white corridors, with a white figure on either side of me, holding my hands, or holding me down, I could not be sure which.

5

He is lying on a cool table, an aureole of light above him. He tries to focus his eyes, and sees green figures and white figures gathered around him. One of them pricks his arm with a giant needle, all the time murmuring: 'Breathe easily, just breathe easily, and let yourself go.'

And he wants, desperately, to go, but he cannot. Part of him lies inside a soft cloud, part of him remains outside of it, awake, alert.

The voice murmurs to the others.

'You can proceed now.'

He wants to shout: 'No, not yet. Please, not yet. I'm still awake.'

But his lips are paralysed, his limbs are dead, so he can make no movement or noise.

They are in a circle around him, gazing down on him as the scalpel slices through his flesh and his muscles. He feels the cold air of the room rush into the gash that has been opened in him, he feels it pour into him like water into a sinking ship. His blood, loving the knife, surges through his veins towards the opening, dragging the pain behind it. The light above him is wheeling round like a sun gone mad. Green figures, white figures, lights, words, the whole universe is wheeling around in the gravitation of his agony.

Then it stops wheeling, abruptly. He hears a deeper voice.

'What in the name of god is this?'

He struggles again to focus his eyes on a green shape crouched over him. He feels a tugging in the cavity in his body, he feels something sliding out, dragging against the raw organs. Through his bleary, slitted eyes, he sees the figure in green holding something up, displaying it in the still whiteness of the room.

He desperately blinks his eyes to see what those gathered around the table see. The figure in green is holding up, in a pair of calipers, a roll of parchment, dripping blood and pus. The hands that begin carefully to unfurl the parchment are dripping blood and pus too. The deep voice begins reading.

'They were sitting round the fire in the Patagonian darkness, telling stories, as they had done every night all through the voyage south . . .'

The deep voice reads on for a while. Then another voice, a woman's contralto voice, takes up the reading. And after a while, another voice, a soft male northern voice, reads, then another voice, voice after voice, throaty or slurred, sometimes silvery, sometimes with a foreign accent, in all ranges and tones, till the last voice, the deep voice again.

'. . . The resident had snared in the calipers a severed human hand, dripping blood and pus. He was holding it by its thumb, and they could all see, quite clearly, the gold wedding ring on its middle finger and the scarlet polish on the long fingernails.'

There is a long silence around the table. He struggles with his paralysis. He tries desperately to say something, to let them know the truth. But he cannot move, he is a prisoner, bound by his own sinews and ligaments. The deep voice speaks again, pronouncing, as he had feared, his sentence.

'This is a monster. Let us put the parchment back inside him, and leave them together to rot.'

All the figures assembled round that table nod their solemn assent. No one speaks up for him, asks for mercy. He would weep for his own loneliness, for the world's hatred of him. But he has no tears. He sees with what grim energy they bend over him, to finish their task. He tries again to focus his eyes. That hand reaching into him, is it scarred with burn marks? That face looking down at him, does it wear dark glasses, are those lips coloured a violent red? He makes one final effort to summon all his strength. He must explain to them, they must understand. At last, the word that will tell them everything explodes from him.

'NOOOOO!'

6

My own shout woke me up, the echoes of it still vibrating around the room. I was in a cold sweat, my heart trying to tear a hole in my chest. I was embarrassed, thinking I must have wakened the whole hotel. Yet, I could have laughed at the absurdity of my nightmare.

I did what I should have done before going to bed.

I switched on the lamp and got out of bed, onto the cold linoleum floor, regretting my lack of pyjamas (I did take a glance at my belly, just to reassure myself. No, no angular protrusions, no scars). I tiptoed across the room to the upright mahogany coffin that passed as a wardrobe. I swung open the door, and saw the tops of the manila envelopes peeping out of the slit of pocket.

I took the thicker envelope back to bed, and sat with a blanket wrapped around my shoulders. The envelope smelt of the dust of the accumulated years. I pulled out the manuscript, only ten pages or so, fastened together with an old-fashioned wire paper-clip. The paper was of poor quality and a little faded. The title page read:

Notebook, A. McGaw

I turned to the opening page and began to read.

I don't know what I expected, really. Some kind of revelation, perhaps, a key to the mystery of Zachary and all the other Mackenzies. And at first glance, I thought I might have found what I had been looking for. The notes were about the Mackenzies. But a brief glance through them showed they would be of little help. They made no mention of the murder, or its effects on the children. The fast is, they were more like preliminary notes for fictional characters than coherent descriptions of real people. I tried to read the four sketches again, but I couldn't, this time, get past even the first lines: 'At the age of eight Amos Mackenzie was consigned to "The Abbey," a home for waifs and strays . . .' My eyes wouldn't stay open. The prose of Zachary Mackenzie was a splendid antidote to insomnia.

I laid the pages on the bedside table, switched off the lamp, snuggled back into the rough womb of hotel blankets. I yawned the requisite number of yawns and, this time, so far as I remember, slept my usual, preferred, dreamless sleep.

7

Home again, and Helen was happy with her gift, especially with the inscription at the front. She would quote it over and over again: 'I am not I: pity the tale of me.' She showed me, too, what I had not noticed, on the title page of the book: *Printed by Rbt Jaggarde, and are to be soulde at the sign of The Boar, London 1599*. Just such coincidences as this always delighted us.

When we made love that first night back in my apartment, I realized that it was her solidity that I loved so much. To touch her hard nipples, to press the tight coils of her pubic hair, to slide slowly into her, to smell her body was to school myself in the reality of substance. We spoke then our own, intimate language, used a vocabulary that required the intertwining of our tongues.

We lay back, looking out through the picture window at the clear night sky, speculating, as we often did, upon what shapes would appear if we were to connect the star-dots.

Could that be the Big Dipper in the north-east? Helen thought it was. I saw only an ornate letter P. Despite our disagreements, we always took comfort in our ignorance, for the sky through this window was *our* sky, no matter how mysterious.

One thing puzzled me. Unlike the previous occasions, Helen had shown hardly any interest in my meeting with Isabel Jaggard and the story of the death of Zachary Mackenzie. I had tried, several times, to give her more details, to expound my theories on Archie McGaw. But she seemed to want to avoid the subject. When I told her about Cromarty's view that he expected soon to resolve the case of the Mackenzie family, she did not show any surprise that I had never told her he was involved. She looked at me as though she had been only half-listening or didn't wish to hear what I was saying. Till she looked at me and said:

'So it won't be long till we all know where we are.'

I loved her too much to ask her what she meant. But that night, I decided the time was right for our trip to the Paradise Motel.

8

The Paradise Motel. We always thought of it as our refuge. The building itself was not imposing, a white clapboard structure on the rugged east coast. The owner, a small withdrawn man, trusted us. The maid, a jovial woman, never interrupted us. We invariably took the same room, a plain, white room, with a little balcony looking out to the ocean. Now, in the off-season (we regarded the off-season as our season), when the motel was deserted, all we asked was that our room be warm and clean. We did not need the restaurant. When we wanted to eat, we would drive north into the town, a few miles away. That was the way we preferred it, using the motel as our base.

Winter was well on its way, and we knew it might snow any day. It was a good time for walking along the beach, smelling the cold, salt air, or climbing among the treeless hills of the coast, so like the hills of other places. On the beach, we would often find pieces of flotsam clothed in seaweed so thick we could not tell what was inside. I would slash it open with my knife to reveal the true identities.

On our third morning there, as we were putting on our coats to go for a walk, the phone rang.

'Ezra, sorry to disturb you. This is Donald Cromarty speaking. May I come and see you, right away?'

This time, I was surprised, to say the least, but polite. I asked him where he was calling from. He said he was only half an hour away, down the coast. He didn't want to talk on the phone. What else could I do? I told him, by all means, to come to the hotel as soon as he could.

I could hardly believe he was so near. I had taken comfort in the thought that he, above all, was thousands of mile away. I had told no one else we were at the Paradise

Motel. We never told anyone about our visits here. So how could he have tracked me down?

I had no doubt why he wanted to see me. The final resolution. He wanted to present it to me, personally. I tried to take comfort in what one part of my mind was telling me again and again: don't worry, how will he be able to tell the truth and save himself? Surely his desire to survive will keep him quiet?

Helen slipped on her coat to go walking on the beach. She felt it would be better to leave Cromarty and me alone. As she went to the door, I put the sad question to her.

'Did you tell him we were coming to the Paradise Motel?'

And she came to me and kissed me so softly I hardly felt her lips.

'I am not I: pity the tale of me,' she said. Or, at least, I think that is what she said, for she spoke so quietly I was not sure of her words. Then she was gone.

9

So Cromarty found me sitting in my room alone, sipping a glass of whisky. Our handshake was only to establish the distance between us. Despite the fact he had come from the sea-air, outside, he brought no odour with him. His face seemed younger to me than when we had last met. That made no difference, for his purpose was old, and deadly. He sat down, unasked.

'Well. It's all over. I can tell you the facts quite simply, now that my inquiries are complete. They are as follows. No expedition ship named the *Mingulay* carried a party to Patagonia, at the turn of the century or any other time. No doctor named Mackenzie murdered his wife. No children named Mackenzie, the offspring of such a doctor, were sent to orphanages. No Holy Order of Correction, as the so-called Archie McGaw names it in his so-called *Notebook*, ever existed.'

I might have objected strongly. I might have challenged his version of the facts. I might have suggested that it was surely a little naïve on the part of a scholar such as himself to place such faith in the simple matter of names. I might have asked him how he could possibly know what was in the *Notebook*, when I had not yet sent it to him. But what would have been the use?

'No record exists of a Doctor Yerdeli, or of an Institute for the Lost. Extensive checking has shown that no one with the initials JP was ever the owner of a large newspaper in this country. It has been established that no Pablo Renowsky, ex-boxer or other, ever lived in the town of Xtecal. No such town exists.'

I might have said never mind all that. That kind of thing anybody may challenge. But what about Isabel Jaggard? You heard her yourself. Have you no faith even in your own eyes and ears But common sense is wasted on a man determined to destroy himself.

'No Daniel Stevenson ever worked at a mine in Muirton. Muirton itself does not exist. As for you, Ezra Stevenson, your name is not registered at the university at which you say we were old friends. There are no records anywhere of the people you have called Daniel Stevenson, John and Elizabeth Stevenson, Joanna Stevenson, Isabel Jaggard, Gib Douglas, Angus Cameron, Amos Mackenzie, Rachel Mackenzie, Esther Mackenzie, and Zachary Mackenzie. Absolutely no records. In addition, your reports are a mishmash of anachronisms and impossibilities.'

I might have given him one last chance. I might have pleaded outright: But, Cromarty. You yourself were there in the The Last Minstrel. You heard, with your own ears, about Zachary Mackenzie, and how he became Archie McGaw, and burned. You were there. I was there.

'No. Whoever you are, I have never met you before in all my life.'

I suppose I might still have gone on, looking innocent, denying everything, placing the burden of proof on him.

But I did not. He was the kind of man who was not only willing to accept the logical consequences of his pedantic notion of truth, but who would insist upon them as his right. And I had known that about him, from the very start. He was waiting for me to ask the question he had been goading me to ask all along, the question that would prove him right.

I had my truth, too, to uphold. So I asked what I had to ask.

'What about you, then, Cromarty? If none of those

others exist, if none of those things happened, where does that leave you, my friend?'

Because, all at once, I was sick of the whole thing, weary of keeping company with such demanding, ungrateful people, all of them depending upon me for their lives and their deaths, absorbing me limb by limb, making me feel so insubstantial, I hardly knew if I existed, myself, any more.

10

After Cromarty was gone, I felt like a man ready to begin recovering from a long illness. If only I could have talked to Helen: I needed to tell her how everything ended. If I could have done that, I would have felt better. But I knew she would never come back from her walk. So what was there to do but fill up my glass, and perhaps weep a little (if a man responsible for so much suffering may weep) at the frailty of love.

He is dozing, sitting in a wicker chair on a balcony on the Paradise Motel. The squat, clapboard building looks out across a beach onto the North Atlantic Ocean, a grey ocean on a grey day. The man is wearing a heavy tweed overcoat, gloves, and a scarf. When he opens his eyes, as he does from time to time, he can see for miles to where the grey water meets the slightly less grey sky. Today, he thinks, this ocean might easily be a huge handwritten manuscript covered as far as the eye can see with regular lines of neat, cursive writing. At the bottom, near the shore, the lines are clearer, and he keeps thinking it might be possible to make out what they say. Then, crash! they break up, on pale brown sand, on black rocks, on the pitted remains of an old concrete jetty. The words, whatever they were, dissolve into white foam on the beach.

SIMON LOUVISH

City of Blok

The City of Jerusalem, November 1977. Avram Blok, failed emigre, useless citizen and evader of all causes, is about to be released from the State Mental Hospital into a Middle East due to be redeemed by the Camp David Peace treaty. Alas, the City of Blok is not one to take the threat of a quiet life idly! Riven by social, political and religious schisms, the City girds itself for a resumption of its millenial agonies: mad Rabbis, corrupt politicians, trapped dreamers, resurrected historical figures living way past their allotted time, crowd and battle their way through the streets of the centripetal Capital of the modern State of Israel, watched over by the shadowy, ever present Department of Apocalyptic Affairs . . .

'(Simon Louvish) has probably anticipated – better than anyone outside Israel – further madness to come.'

Bryan Cheyette, *Times Literary Supplement*

Flamingo

LAWRENCE NAUMOFF

The Night of the Weeping Women

'One of the most endearing books about family life ever penned . . . This book is Lawrence Naumoff's debut as a novelist and it is a remarkable one . . . Funny, sad, heartwarming, it tickles like the fizz of a peanut-spiked Dr. Pepper.' *Washington Post Book World*

'A disturbing and unsettling piece of fiction . . . The piling up of revelation after revelation makes for enormous cumulative power . . . Naumoff writes strong scenes as funny as they are painful.' *New York Newsday*

'Dark, powerful . . . The style is as homey as deep-dish apple pie, the subject-matter as treacherous as an unlit street . . . This vivid, commanding novel scorches into your mind, on its every page, the fact that once you have stopped loving you can never begin again.' *Sunday Times*

Flamingo

Flamingo

Flamingo is a quality imprint publishing both fiction and non-fiction. Below are some recent titles.

Fiction

☐ Punishments *Francis King* £3.99
☐ The Therapy of Avram Blok *Simon Louvish* £4.99
☐ A Sense of Touch *Christopher Osborn* £4.99
☐ Life With a Star *Jiri Weil* £4.99
☐ The Way We Lived Then *Woodrow Wyatt* £3.99
☐ Emily L *Marguerite Duras* £3.99
☐ Dexterity *Douglas Bauer* £4.99
☐ The Towers of Trebizond *Rose Macaulay* £4.50
☐ The Ultimate Good Luck *Richard Ford* £3.99
☐ The Public World of Parable Jones *Dominic Behan* £3.99

Non-fiction

☐ The Rites of Autumn *Dan O'Brien* £3.99
☐ Oil Notes *Rick Bass* £3.99
☐ In Xanadu *William Dalrymple* £4.99
☐ Home Life (Book Four) *Alice Thomas Ellis* £3.99

You can buy Flamingo paperbacks at your local bookshop or newsagent. Or you can order them from Fontana Paperbacks, Cash Sales Department, Box 29, Douglas, Isle of Man. Please send a cheque, postal or money order (not currency) worth the purchase price plus 22p per book (or plus 22p per book if outside the UK).

NAME (Block letters)_____

ADDRESS_____

_____

_____